THE ENGLISH WITCH

Also by Loretta Chase:

ISABELLA

THE ENGLISH WITCH

Loretta Chase

Walker and Company
New York

First published in the United States of America in 1988 by the Walker Publishing Company, Inc.

Library of Congress Cataloging-in-Publication Data

Chase, Loretta Lynda, 1949–
    The English witch/Loretta Chase.
        p.   cm.
    ISBN 0-8027-1027-1
    I. Title.
PS3553.H3347E5   1988   813'.54—dc19   87-35096

Published simultaneously in Canada by Thomas Allen & Son Canada, Limited, Markham, Ontario.

Printed in the United States of America

10 9 8 7 6 5 4 3 2 1

Prologue

"WELL, MARIA, WHAT do you think?"

Lady Deverell looked up from the letter she'd just finished reading, but her gaze went to the fire, rather than to her questioner. Though it was a bright, cozy fire, so comforting on this late winter evening, she sighed. "How cleverly she writes. But then, I daresay she inherited her scholarly Papa's intellect."

"Well, it wasn't from her Mama, that's for certain. Juliet, rest her soul, was a beautiful giddypate. A more ill-suited pair one could scarcely imagine. Juliet would never budge from London, and Charles was determined to be abroad. So, what happens but Alexandra is left with a governess and one or two servants in that lonely little place in the country. She was neglected shamefully, to my way of thinking—and now this. If only she had confided the matter sooner, I might have done something before she went away with her Papa. Wretched man." Lady Bertram nodded balefully at the letter, as though it were Sir Charles Ashmore himself.

Certainly, if it were—and if it had had any sensibilities at all—it would have crept away in mortification. A tall, full-figured woman of sixty or so, unbowed by age or infirmity, the Countess Bertram could, when she liked, make herself very intimidating to lesser mortals.

All the same, the letter lay, oblivious to the countess's scorn, in Lady Deverell's delicate hand. Nor was the languid owner of that hand intimidated. She, in fact, scarcely

1

seemed to attend at all, so absentmindedly did she answer. "Yes, it is most tiresome. And yet they are so very far away. Albania. One can hardly think how to help her at this great distance."

"Nonetheless, one must. She's my goddaughter and requires my help. We must cudgel our brains, Maria."

"Oh, must we?" Lady Deverell sounded rather faint at the prospect, as though someone had proposed that she run from London to Brighton. "Oh, dear, I suppose we must. Well, let me see." She glanced down at the letter. "There is the money, of course. Though one cannot understand why Charles went to a wool merchant for financial backing."

"Because he is a proud, obstinate creature, who'd sooner shoot himself than 'toady to that bunch of aristocratic halfwits,' as he calls the Society of Dilettanti. So what does he do but put all his affairs into the hands of George Burnham—who was sly enough to toady to *him*."

"But it is only money, after all, and you have enough, certainly—"

"Yes, yes, I tried" was the impatient reply. "The day I received the letter, I dispatched a bank draft to Burnham. It came back with a curt note informing me that he could accept no funds on Ashmore's behalf without Ashmore's approval. Now Burnham has begun pressing for the marriage—and of course you see why."

Lady Deverell gave the letter another glance and sighed. "Ah, yes. The eldest daughter is nearly one-and-twenty and must make her comeout before she is obliged to wear caps."

"A pack of mushrooms, Maria. Why should the Burnhams care for my money when they might use Alexandra to introduce those ignorant, encroaching girls to society?"

Lady Deverell made vaguely sympathetic murmurs.

"I cannot think what to do next. For all her humourous comments, it's plain Alexandra is distressed. But if I write to her father, he'll resent my interference and, in one of his headstrong passions, is liable to haul them before one of those dervishes, to be married there. Really, he's the most vexing man."

Lady Bertram's companion, immovably unvexed, replied dreamily, "Yes. Matters seem to have reached a crisis. Your goddaughter has run out of strategems, and the Burnhams press her Papa. Dear, dear. So he is determined to be back in England by summer."

"Yes, and there's the devil of it. He'll pack her off to Yorkshire as soon as they set foot in the kingdom, and the poor girl will be married before she can blink."

"How fatiguing to think of so much energy expended to such ill purpose. Yet that is exactly what he must do." Lady Deverell's preoccupied gaze wandered to the clock on the mantelpiece. "Unless, of course, some complication should intervene."

"Yes." A faint smile softened the countess's patrician features.

Lady Deverell followed another bored sigh with a change of subject. "Dear me, what a dreary winter this has been with half the world in Brussels. But it is nearly over. I understand Basil Trevelyan plans to return from Greece by summer."

"Yes. So he's written."

"Well, that will be pleasant, will it not? After three years we shall all be glad to see him."

"Oh, yes. Prodigious glad."

"I wonder," Lady Deverell mused, her eyes still on the clock, "what he will think of Albania."

"Albania, my dear? Is that where he means to go?" the countess asked, very innocently.

"Why, yes, Clementina. Now I think of it, that must be *exactly* what he intends."

1

I⊤ WAS CALLED the "City of a Thousand Stairs." From a distance, the white stone houses with their elaborate red roofs appeared to be carved out of the mountainside itself. They were white fairy stairs, zigzagging their way up to the mediaeval citadel. Veiled by the early dawn mist, Gjirokastra seemed exactly the sort of place where evil sorcerers held fair princesses captive.

On closer view the houses—windowless on the first floor, bay-windowed and ornate on the upper stories—were miniature fortresses themselves, clustered about their majestic parent. And at this hour of morning there were no fairies, princesses, nor evil sorcerers. There were instead a few women, most of them dressed in black, soberly going about their chores.

The town was founded, according to folk legend, by a princess named Argjiro; but Sir Charles believed that its name came from the Illyrian tribe of Argyres that had settled nearby. Gjirokastra's recent history was less mysterious: like every other town and hamlet of Albania, it had known only rare intervals of peace since its founding. Just four years ago, in 1811, Ali Pasha Tepelena had bombarded the rebellious town with artillery.

In time, it could expect to be bombarded again by somebody, for some reason, but now in the misty dawn of what promised to be another sweltering June day, the place was quiet.

Occasionally the women of Gjirokastra spoke to one

another, but mainly they attended to their work. Certainly they had better things to do than watch the departure of the small caravan. The English were leaving, they knew. They also knew why.

The women of Gjirokastra did not approve of "Skandara" Ashmore. Women were supposed to go about their back-breaking labour quietly, troubling nobody, but this English witch troubled everybody. Too many yearning songs had been composed in tribute to her green, sorceress eyes and gleaming dark curls. She made the young men restless, and that was bad.

Meanwhile, the small caravan descending to the valley was not quite so subdued as the sleepy town it had just left. Alexandra Ashmore had not given up trying to sidetrack her father. This endeavour had grown increasingly difficult, because he'd finally made up his mind to go home, and once he made up his mind to something, he tended to apply all the concentration he normally focussed on ancient inscriptions. At present his course was fixed. A certain Albanian family's apologetic warning the previous day had merely hastened a departure planned months before.

"But Papa," Alexandra was saying, as calmly as she could, "surely we cannot come so close to Butrint and not spend time there."

"I can go later, after you and Randolph are married."

"But think of the expense. To go all the way back to England and then return all the way here again."

"We've delayed long enough. You must be married. In a few more years, you'll be too old to have children. Randolph will want a family."

Glancing ahead at the young man who rode with their ragged guard, Stefan, and their slightly less ragged drago-man, Gjergi, Alexandra privately took leave to differ with her father. Randolph's beloved family existed already, in the remnants of ancient times. Her fiancé lusted for scraps of buildings and fragments of sculpture as another man might lust for women. He was blind even to her own charms. And she, while not vain, was not stupid either. She knew that most men found her very attractive.

Randolph had agreed to marry her because he was dimly aware that he had to marry somebody. His father obligingly had found him a bride, thereby saving Randolph the trouble of looking for one, so he was content. Actually, oblivious was more like it. But aloud she said only, "Why, we can be married next year. Four-and-twenty is not the very brink of senility. And Randolph wouldn't mind. He, too, wishes to explore Butrint."

"No. There'll always be trouble until you're married. Today we leave Gjirokastra because Dhimitri Musolja's besotted with you. In another place, it'll be someone else. With these men chasing you and upsetting their families, we accomplish nothing."

That much was true. This was the fifth town they'd been forced to leave because of amourous young men. At any rate, it was futile to argue when those stubborn lines settled into Papa's forehead. Later she'd try again. She'd tempt him with Butrint once more.

Gjirokastra, nestled in the mountains of southern Albania, was mainly mediaeval, although pieces of ancient rubble formed part of the material of which the citadel was built, and there were traces of ancient settlements nearby. Butrint was another story. Marcus Tullius Cicero had written of it, and according to the *Aeneid*, it was founded by the Trojans on their way from Troy to Italy. Though Papa said that was mere legend, he was dying to explore the place, as was Randolph. Surely there must be some way to convince them to stay—just a while longer. And perhaps, while they investigated antiquities, she might have an answer to the letter she'd written so many months ago.

But what could Aunt Clem do, after all? Mama had adamantly objected to the match with Randolph; but as soon as she passed away, Papa had settled everything with George Burnham. While Papa had arranged the marriage as a means of paying off his long-standing debt to the wool merchant, he honestly believed he was looking out for his daughter's best interests. Her dowry was insignificant, and he had nothing to leave her after his death. Without a husband, her future would be a grim one.

Awake to the need for a husband, she'd convinced her parents to scrape together enough money for a Season. Unfortunately, though she attracted many suitors, her lack of fortune as well as her Papa's eccentricity had a dampening effect on Honourable Intentions. The few London bachelors whose sensibilities were not thus dampened were unendurable. Alexandra did not think herself, as Mama complained, excessively fastidious, but it was quite impossible to accept Mr. Courtland, who was sixty, or Sir Alfred, who was short and fat and practically illiterate, or Mr. Porter, a Pink of the Ton whose only real passion was his tailor.

In short, when, near the Season's end, her Mama had contracted a fever and died, Alexandra remained unclaimed. George Burnham was on the spot immediately, urging that the match go forward at once. Alexandra had responded by reminding her father that she was in mourning and convincing him to let her spend the time with him in Greece. Once they were abroad, it hadn't been difficult to stretch one year into another until six had passed. Papa forgot everything else when he was working.

Meanwhile, she'd occupied herself by helping him keep his sketches and notes in order. She had also learned how to say what was expected of her while her mind wandered elsewhere. Since the two men were generally unaware of her existence, this was no great feat. It was not the most stimulating existence, and she did not see how being married to Randolph would improve it. She would like one day to talk of something besides the Peloponnesian War. With Randolph Burnham, such a day would never come.

While she pondered her past and wondered sadly about her future, the group pressed on in relative silence, broken only by Gjergi's dropping into a soft song about the bravery

7

of the Shqiptar—the Sons of Eagles. The mists that had enshrouded Gjirokastra were giving way to the bright morning sun, when the valley's peace was broken by the thundering of horses' hooves.

Good God. Bandits. Alexandra had scarcely formulated the thought when she saw Stefan and Gjergi reach for the long guns slung across their saddles. Even as they were taking aim, the marauders thundered into their midst, stirring up a choking, blinding storm of dust. Her throat and eyes burning, Alexandra struggled to control her panicked horse with one hand while she fumbled with the other for the pistol tucked into her waistband. In the next instant, she was dragged from her mount and flung onto another. Strong arms gripped her, and she stared up into a laughing, triumphant face.

"Dhimitri!" she gasped.

Furious, she pounded and clawed, screaming at him to let her go. The huge Albanian only laughed and grasped her more tightly.

A single, curt command to his men, and Dhimitri Musolja galloped off with Sir Charles Ashmore's daughter.

Basil Trevelyan glared at the breathtaking prospect beyond the narrow window: green and yellow valley below and majestic peaks beyond. The faint, sweet mountain breeze that cooled the early evening air only made him wish desperately to be home again. After two interminable years in India and another, equally dreary, in Greece, he was as tired of picturesque views as he was tired of business and politics. Now, when he should be on a ship bound for England, he was in Albania, in a wretched mountain village, whose suspicious inhabitants would tell him nothing.

He turned angrily to the letters on the rough table before him. They'd come to him, one folded over the other, in Greece, and had plagued him ever since. His aunt, of course, habitually ordered him about. That was her character, just as it was his to ignore her. Since she was at least partially responsible for his three-year exile from England, it would have served her right had he torn the cursed things to bits. The trouble was, she knew what she was about. She'd enclosed Miss Ashmore's letter and let that do the business for her. Aunt Clem knew him too well—devious woman.

Basil Trevelyan enjoyed drama. He enjoyed intrigue. And he enjoyed women. He especially enjoyed women, partly for their own sake and partly because relations with them so often involved drama and intrigue—not to mention the obvious pleasures. Because he had excellent taste, he particularly enjoyed beautiful women.

Now here was a "good-looking gel," according to his usually critical aunt, who was attempting to conduct some sort of intrigue of her own. Alexandra Ashmore wrote coolly and humourously, yet movingly, of a typical maiden's plight: her Papa was making her marry a man she didn't love. The bridegroom had the Money. The bride had the Status—the usual trade.

He'd tried one like it himself, three years ago, and had even gone so far as to try to blackmail Isabella Latham into marrying him. He'd failed because not only her relatives but also his own had thwarted him. They'd even had him drugged and abducted to make absolutely certain he couldn't interfere with her marriage to his cousin Edward, Earl of Hartleigh.

Basil was still a bit ashamed of the way he'd behaved. He might not have been quite so ashamed, might even have nursed a grudge, had not Isabella, now Countess of Hartleigh, been the only one to write faithfully to him. Well, she'd always rather liked him. She just hadn't loved him.

How she'd laugh if she could see him now: dirty, unshaven, uncombed, his borrowed clothes ragged and filthy. He was a far cry from the elegant man-about-town she'd known. That sophisticated fellow had been deeply sunk in debt three years ago. Now, thanks to Henry Latham, Basil was rich and even rather a hero—business, as Henry liked to say, being inextricably tied to politics. Having persuaded Basil to work for him, Latham was bound to put the younger man's talent for intrigue to profitable use. Mr. Trevelyan succeeded where even skilled diplomats had failed. For his efforts, he received some modest rewards and generous praise from the Crown. Less modest rewards and fewer words had come from the divers British business-men and Indian princes to whom Basil had proved himself equally invaluable.

Now when he returned to England, he'd be welcome everywhere. Proper Mamas would push their innocent daughters at him. All kinds of respectable young ladies—pretty ones and plain, poor and wealthy and every variety in between—would pursue him. He doubted whether their virginal charms could compete with the more practised arts of the Fashionable Impures he was accustomed to. Still, never loath to be the centre of attention, he looked forward to making the comparison firsthand.

One cleverly written letter had held him back from all that bliss. And why? He had a whim to meet the authoress. If her writing was any sample, she must be a very interest-ing young woman.

That was what had brought him to this wretched place. He'd had a hot, miserable journey ending in a miserable town whose sullen folk refused to understand his guide's northern dialect. The name Ashmore evoked nothing but stubborn incomprehension.

Basil ran his fingers through his tangled hair. The tawny, sun-bleached mane badly wanted cutting. His amber eyes were dull with exhaustion, and as he thought of more days wasted in search of the missing Ashmores, his head began throbbing horribly. Blast them! And blast his aunt as well. He wanted to be home in his own clothes and clean again. He wanted a familiar bed and familiar food. He thought longingly of London's cooling drizzles, forgetting that the city would soon be hot and odoriferous. He yearned for the quiet, cool comfort of his club. He even recalled wistfully the rustic peace of Hartleigh Hall.

While he was in the midst of tormenting himself with these reflexions, Gregor crept into the room. "Zotir Vasil," he whispered.

Basil awoke from his reverie and gazed stupidly at his dragoman. "What? What is it?"

"We have found Zotir Ashmore. A local boy, Dhimitri Musolja, has taken the girl."

"Taken her? Where?"

"Here, in the town, to his father's house. We must go quickly. There is big trouble now and soon, maybe worse."

Alexandra's Albanian was not very fluent, but then, it was a difficult language. Papa theorised that it was traceable to the ancient Illyrian tongue, preserved, despite repeated foreign conquests, out of sheer obstinacy. For instance, while the Turks had held the country in an undependable state of submission since the death of the great Albanian patriot Skanderbeg, in the fifteenth century, only a handful of Turkish words had been absorbed. Albanian was Albanian still, and its inflexions were Alexandra's despair. Nonetheless, though her speech could send her woman-servant, the jovial Lefka, into fits of laughter, Alexandra's understanding was quite good. Certainly she comprehended enough to follow the arguments going on in the room above.

The debate had continued all day, and their voices carried easily down to the shed where she waited, because they hadn't troubled to lower them. The father demanded that the English girl be returned to her father. The brothers shouted about shame and disgrace. Even the mother pleaded with her favourite, her youngest son, while the other women of the household complained that the English girl was a witch. Had she not been forced to leave Tepelena because she made the young men crazy?

So the battle had raged while the English witch sat on the dirt floor of a shed that smelled strongly of goats, and tried to understand why men were so pigheaded. There was her normally logical Papa forcing two incompatible and unenthusiastic persons into marriage. Here was Dhimitri trying to force her to marry *him*. How on earth had she imagined Aunt Clem could help her out of such a pickle?

Morning heated up into afternoon, and afternoon darkened into dusk while the family battled on. The odds were against Dhimitri, but he was spoiled and headstrong. A while ago, he'd raved that if his family would not accept Skandara as his wife, he'd go away with her to live among strangers. He'd go, he shouted, to Pogradeç, and make his living by fishing in the lake. His mother shrieked. His father screamed at him to go and be damned, and the others made a deafening chorus. Then, suddenly, everything was still. She heard new voices break the silence. Her spirits rose, only to sink again. They were not familiar voices.

What if Papa and Randolph had been hurt . . . or killed, all because of a young man she'd thought was content to gaze adoringly at her as he sang his mournful little love songs. Who'd have guessed he'd dare abduct the daughter of Ali Pasha's honoured guest? Evidently he respected the great Pasha as little as he did the mourning Alexandra still wore. Lefka had promised that would keep the men at a respectful distance, but it hadn't.

Now nothing short of a miracle could save Alexandra from marrying the hotheaded youth. She'd be treated as a servant, a pack animal. She'd have to submit to his hot, eager embraces—and have his children! God help her, she'd kill herself first. She'd throw herself from a ledge. In Gjirokastra, after all, there were ledges aplenty.

A more delicate female than Alexandra Ashmore might have given way to tears. Certainly she had reason enough, but she refused to cry despite the horrible ache in her throat. She was wishing for her pistol—shooting herself was preferable to hurtling down from a precipice—when the door creaked open.

It was one of Dhimitri's brothers. She didn't know which, there being seven plus innumerable sisters, all of whom looked alike. Dhimitri stood out mainly because he was the giant of the family and understood a little English. This brother was ordering her to follow him.

He led her up into the house proper and on to the large, sparsely furnished room where the family was accustomed to gather and were all gathered now: parents, siblings, spouses, and divers aunts and uncles. There was, moreover, another Albanian she didn't know, speaking in the dialect of the north, and another man whose hair was sun-bleached gold. He must also come from the north, where so much of the population was fair, though his costume resembled nothing she'd seen before, north or south. For a moment, in the room's dim light, he seemed a golden Macedonian, like those who centuries ago had swept down from the mountains. As he turned his tanned, beautifully sculpted face towards her, she noted that his eyes were very unusual. Amber, with a slight upward slant, they reminded her of the eyes of a cat.

They were watchful, too, like a cat's eyes. As they lit upon her, the expression turned to one of joyful recognition, and she was astonished to hear him cry in cultured British accents, "Alexandra, my love, you are safe."

Before she had time to think how to react, he crossed the room, threw his arms around her, and crushed her to him. The suddenness of the onslaught made her gasp, but sensing quickly the role she was to play, she took her lead from him and returned his hug with feigned enthusiasm. His ironic smile made her blush as he drew away from her to gesture towards their suspicious audience.

"My darling, I have been trying to explain to these good people that I am your own Basil, your betrothed, come at last to take you home to be my wife. The trouble is Gregor cannot make himself understood, and that angry young man over there"—he indicated an enraged Dhimitri, now being held back by three brothers—"seems to think that you are *his* intended bride. Would you, my sweet, be kind enough to explain to them how it is with us?"

Though it was a tad daunting to have what seemed like a hundred pairs of suspicious eyes fixed upon her, she began, in Albanian even more halting than usual. She was not quite sure what she said—nor were the members of the clan, as they tried to puzzle out her bizarre grammatical constructions—but it was something about being promised to each other for years.

Though the others appeared satisfied with this incoherent babble, a red-faced Dhimitri demanded to know why her father claimed she was promised to that other one. He meant, of course, Mr. Burnham. In response, Alexandra promptly invented some nonsense about Basil's early poverty, and how he'd gone to seek his fortune. Basil smiled as his dragoman translated this with some difficulty, for she told the truth, all unwittingly. She went on to explain how she'd promised to wait for him. Her Papa wanted her to marry Mr. Burnham, but she didn't want Mr. Burnham. Now, she told them, as she gazed up at Basil with what she hoped was a look of adoration, her own true love had come for her as he'd promised. There was more murmuring, as the assembled audience struggled with her garbled prose, and then there were sounds of agreement.

Her would-be fiancé now turned to her with a look of such passionate longing that she was momentarily breathless. "I think, my love," he said softly, "that the parents are happy to believe in our star-crossed love. But Dhimitri wants convincing." As though unable to contain his feelings another moment, Basil wrapped his arms around her and kissed her.

It was not the make-believe kiss Alexandra was expecting, but a long, deep, dizzyingly thorough kiss that, when he'd finally done, left her stunned, overwarm, and breathing very hard.

Basil, meanwhile, was persuading himself that Dhimitri was still sceptical. Miss Ashmore was an uncommonly attractive young woman, surprisingly curvaceous under that shapeless black rag she wore. Though her chestnut curls were matted and her face was smudged with dirt and she did smell faintly of goats, he tightened his arms around her, preparatory to supplying more conclusive evidence.

Dhimitri's anguished cry stopped him. *"Mjaft!"* the young man wailed. *"Mjaft! Merre dhe largoju prej meje!"*

Basil looked at Alexandra questioningly.

"He says, 'Enough,' and tells you to take me and go."

"That's a mercy," was the muttered reply.

With one arm still about Miss Ashmore's lovely shoulders, Basil hurried her out of the house.

2

"I'M SORRY I could not procure another horse on such short notice, Miss Ashmore. You'll have to ride with me. But I promise I won't fling you across the saddle."

Too emotionally drained to reply, she let him lift her onto the mount. They rode for some minutes with Gregor behind them, before she recovered sufficiently to ask where they were going.

"To meet up with your father. This business called for cool heads, and Gregor persuaded him to await us in the next village. I'm afraid that means we've a night's ride ahead of us. At any rate, they're all safe—including your horse. Not that I'd have any objections to continuing our present mode of travel the whole way to Prevesa."

His breath was warm at her neck, and his low, coaxing tone made her feel a little anxious. It was dark, and both these men were strangers. But she was too tired to be truly frightened.

"At this point, sir, I shouldn't care whether I was flung across the saddle or trudging behind. So long as I can get free of this horrid town." She turned to look at him. "Who are you, anyway?"

"Your fiancé, silly girl."

"Yes." She brushed this away. "That was very clever of you, but who are you really—and what brings you to Gjirokastra? The English rarely go beyond the coastal cities."

"Ah, yes. The country, according to Gibbon, 'within sight of Italy is less known than the interior of America.' "

"You've read Gibbon?" she asked, in some surprise.

"Yes, but I got my quote from *Childe Harold*. If it wasn't what Gibbon said or Gibbon who said it, we must blame Byron for yet something else. But that is neither here nor there. My name—in answer to one question—is Basil Trevelyan. I am here—in answer to the other question—because Aunt Clem told me I must come and get you. And Aunt Clem, as you must know, is always to be obeyed."

"Aunt Clem? You mean Lady Bertram?"

"Yes."

"Good heavens! She sent you all the way here—but I never meant—" She bit her lip. She *had* meant—or hoped—after all, that Lady Bertram would perform a miracle. And here it—or he—was.

"It was not so great a distance, Miss Ashmore. I happened to be in Greece—or what one assumes is Greece, though you can hardly tell nowadays."

"So Lady Bertram wrote to you. Then you must know something of my story."

"Oh, yes." He didn't think it worth mentioning that her letter now reposed in the pocket of his worn cloak. "Of course, I was puzzled concerning what I could do to help you. My skills do not lie in coaxing parents out of marital arrangements for their offspring. But I have, as Aunt Clem knows, a weakness for intrigue, and the challenge appealed to me. So, here I am."

Though it was rather embarrassing that he knew of her plight, her sense of humour soon came to the fore. It was a ridiculous plight, was it not? With a rueful smile she said, "Still, you did not expect, I think, to have to rescue me from abductors."

"No, I hadn't anticipated adventures—but then, 'Fierce are Albania's children,' according to Byron. Shall I expect more adventures, Miss Ashmore? I wouldn't mind a little warning."

"Good heavens, I should hope not. I can't think what possessed Dhimitri."

"You can't?" His voice grew softer. "How odd, for I can. Yet he gallantly gave you up to your own true love. One gathers that he did not think Mr. Burnham your own true love."

"I suppose you're right. Dhimitri did insist that he was rescuing me."

"Then bless his romantic heart. He believed the show we put on for him—and he's given me an idea."

Since it was most unlikely she'd fall off a horse proceeding at this slow pace, Miss Ashmore wondered why, as they conversed, he felt it necessary to press so close. Or why he must lower his voice to that insinuating timbre when there was only the dragoman to hear. She was unable at the moment to devise a polite way to put these questions to him, considering he'd just saved her from a Fate Worse Than Death. Instead, she asked what idea he had.

"I may have hit upon a way to confound your father's plans for your future. Was he in London during your one Season?"

"No, he came back only just before Mama passed away, at the end of June."

"Then he doesn't know I wasn't in London either. In that case, suppose you formed an attachment then, which you've kept secret all this time—for precisely the reasons we gave Dhimitri and his family."

"An attachment? But what—oh, I see. You think to convince Papa . . ." She trailed off, wondering why the idea made her uneasy.

"That your heart is otherwise engaged."

"I doubt it will make any difference. He's very set on Mr. Burnham."

"Ah, but he hasn't even met me yet, Miss Ashmore. Shall I tell you my credentials?" Without waiting for a reply, he began to enumerate his advantages in ringing tones that made Gregor sit up and take notice. While Basil himself had no title, his first cousin was the seventh Earl of Hartleigh. Furthermore, the Trevelyan family could be traced back to Norman times. His Aunt Clem, daughter of an earl, had maintained her status by marrying the Earl of Bertram, whose own line was equally ancient and honourable.

"Moreover," Basil went on, "in addition to being monstrous well connected, I am now quite plump in the pocket—which makes me a perfectly unexceptionable catch. Add to these my considerable charm and a reputed talent for making black appear white—and I cannot imagine any Papa saying me nay."

"But what of your character, sir?" Alexandra asked sternly, imitating her father at his stuffiest. "Mr. Burnham is honest as the day is long, a dedicated scholar and a gentleman, an earnest and honourable man."

"Deuce take it—you have me out there, madam. You see, my character is as black as black can be. I am an incorrigible liar, a wastrel, and—I beg your pardon, ma'am, but the truth must be told—a womaniser. Selfish and fickle, I am, as Aunt Clem will be quick to tell you, a perfectly dreadful boy."

Alexandra was able to suppress her gasp, but couldn't help turning to look at him in disbelief. The dreadful boy was smiling at her so angelically that she couldn't tell whether he was roasting her or not.

"Well then," she answered, careful to keep her voice light, "you'd better not tell Papa that."

"Of course not. I am a liar, after all. And a very good one, too, I might add."

Doubtless he was. He'd made such a good show of a passionate embrace that even now, thinking back on it, she felt a little dizzy. But then, what did she know of such things? One or two gentlemen had stolen kisses from her, but those were hasty affairs, easily halted by the simple expedient of stomping on a highly polished boot.

To have employed like measures in his case would have

meant disaster. Consequently, his was the first full-length kiss she'd experienced. She wasn't sure whether she'd liked it or not. There had been a rush of sensation not altogether unpleasant. That sensation had made her feel powerless, and the loss of control frightened her. Though not nearly as large as Dhimitri—not even so very many inches taller than herself—Mr. Trevelyan was alarmingly strong. She was by no means a frail little thing, and yet it had seemed he might easily crush her to pieces if he liked. Now, as he held her too close, too tightly, she was acutely conscious of his lean, muscular form and of a tension between them that made her breath come and go more rapidly than usual.

"Well then, will I do?" His voice dropped to a whisper again, and his mouth seemed terribly close to her ear.

Fortunately, she'd had some experience with flirtatious gentlemen, a species of which Basil Trevelyan appeared to be a member.

Taking herself firmly in hand, Alexandra answered with cool dignity. "I suppose you must, since there is no one else, Mr. Trevelyan. However, I am puzzled why you must hold me so tight. I assure you I am in no danger of falling off your horse. Unless you think to begin the performance already. But Papa is still miles away, so there really is no need."

"I was practising, Miss Ashmore," came the amused reply.

"I doubt you require any practice. You have quite convinced me of your aptitude for this sort of thing."

"Then perhaps *you* want practice," he persisted.

"I had much rather you trusted me to muddle along. I promise to follow your lead exactly."

He gave a forlorn sigh. "Which is all to say you don't trust me a bit. And after all we've been to each other. Cruel girl. I am yours to command." He loosened his hold on her. "There. Is that better?"

"Yes, thank you."

"Well, it seems a great deal worse to me. Let me know if you change your mind."

"There is very little likelihood of that. Now perhaps you'd be kind enough to change the subject."

"Heartless girl. You forbid me to hold you, and then you forbid me even to flirt with you. This is quite the worst engagement I've ever experienced."

"Ah, then you've been engaged before, Mr. Trevelyan?"

"Very briefly."

The terse reply and the tense silence that followed told her she'd inadvertently stumbled upon an interesting topic. He gave her only a moment to ponder this little mystery before he went on, in a more normal voice, to ask what had brought the Ashmores to Albania.

Alexandra explained that they'd come at the express invitation of Ali Pasha himself. Evidently, when Byron had visited, either he or Mr. Hobhouse had mentioned Sir Charles's work to the great Pasha of Egypt. Ali, being an Albanian and in a humour at the time to cultivate the English, had graciously invited the scholar to explore the little-known country.

"And Dhimitri dared to abduct the daughter of Ali Pasha's honoured guest?"

"The Albanians are afraid of nothing, Mr. Trevelyan. It is fortunate you were so inventive. Papa is no diplomat and might very well have threatened them with Ali. They would have promptly taken Dhimitri's part and laughed at the danger, because the Albanians are not only fearless, but proud and clannish as well. Once Ali got to hear of it— he hears of everything, you know, for all that he's in Egypt now—he'd send his men to kill everyone in the town just to set an example."

"Yes, I understand he roasts his friends on a spit if they annoy him. Well then, it only goes to show, as I've always maintained, that kisses are infinitely preferable to blood-shed."

She could hardly disagree with this pacifistic opinion,

yet she dared not concur enthusiastically either. It was plain, even from the small sampling he'd provided of his talents, that his charm was, as he claimed, considerable, and she'd rather not have him exert any more of it upon her.

In other circumstances she might have enjoyed a light-hearted flirtation. But there were only the three of them on a dark road, and already his behaviour had been overly civil. He'd been very slow to release his hold on her and was only amused at her reproof. Besides, he'd admitted to being a liar and a womaniser and other dreadful things. While that, too, could be a lie, it was wiser to assume it was not and to be cautious.

She'd appraised Mr. Trevelyan accurately. Nonetheless, she was safer with him than she knew. His conscience, for instance, was an exceedingly feeble one that rarely troubled him. He was, as he'd told her, a womaniser. He was, moreover, feeling exceedingly amourous. He had not held a woman in his arms in many weeks. He had not held an Englishwoman in his arms in over a year. Here was a perfectly acceptable Englishwoman, who, despite the faint redolence of goats, was a perfectly delicious one as well. For all that, Miss Ashmore's virtue was as safe now as if she rode with her own Papa.

While his conscience was to all intents and purposes quite deaf, dumb, and blind, Basil's sense of self-preservation was strong. He wanted to hurry home and wreak havoc with the hearts of London's young ladies. He could not be free to destroy their peace if he were married to this particular young lady; and he knew perfectly well that if he didn't behave himself, he'd have to marry her. Even Basil knew better than to play fast and loose with Aunt Clem's goddaughter. He'd learned, to his cost, what came of antagonising family members. No. The price of pleasure was, in this case, far too high.

These musings on self-preservation led Basil to another problem—one that struck him so forcibly that he abruptly drew back from Miss Ashmore, towards whom he had, rather naturally, been inclining as he meditated. Consequently, she very nearly did fall off the startled horse. Only an excellent sense of balance, nurtured by many long treks on narrow mountain paths, kept her in her place.

"Good heavens!" she cried. "Whatever is the matter?"

"I just thought of something."

"Well, it must be perfectly frightful. Are you trying to kill us both?"

He made no answer to this, being engaged for the moment in soothing his mount and then in soothing Gregor, who had also taken alarm. Only after these two were completely at their ease again did Basil apologise for startling Alexandra.

"I just realised, Miss Ashmore, that if we convince your father of our undying devotion, he'll expect us to marry."

The cold dread with which he uttered the words could not be construed as complimentary. Still, his voice was so chillingly sepulchral that she had to laugh.

She had a very nice laugh—low and husky, like her speaking voice—but Basil was too discomposed to fully appreciate it. Instead, he asked her, with some annoyance, what was so funny.

"You say that as though you expected to be buried alive. How high-strung you are, Mr. Trevelyan. And I wonder that you hadn't thought of it before. Of course Papa would expect us to marry, if he believes this folderol, which I rather doubt."

"Well, then?"

In answer she laughed again.

Basil's survival instincts appeared to have deserted him as he contemplated a few responses that would make her stop laughing—and rather abruptly, at that. He was, in fact, about to take steps towards that end when she spoke in more serious tones.

"Whatever Papa expects, I am not so hen-witted as to marry a perfect stranger simply to be rid of someone else."

"I will not be a perfect stranger by the time we're in England," was the huffy retort.

"Oh, so you mean to make me fall in love with you? That would be asking for trouble."

"That is not at all what I meant, wicked girl."

"Then what *do* you mean?"

He collected himself. Something had gotten in the way of his intellect. Lust, probably. "I meant, my love, only that this is a risky enterprise. I must trust you absolutely to jilt me once we are back, for I cannot, as a gentleman, jilt *you*. If I do, I will be driven away in disgrace—" He was about to say "again," but thought better of it. "My family would never forgive me."

"Yes, of course. There's an etiquette to these things." Her voice was a little tart, but recollecting that he was the only rescuer she had at the moment, she added hastily, "At any rate, I shall not lure you to the altar, Mr. Trevelyan. I solemnly promise to jilt you. In the meantime, if you don't want to give me the wrong idea, I suggest you save your 'my loves' for the appropriate audience."

He took her reproof with more of his natural composure and obediently turned the topic. They settled between them the story that would be told to Sir Charles. Then Mr. Trevelyan's curiosity had to be satisfied.

"How does it happen," he asked, "that we never met? Aunt Clem has godchildren over half England, it seems, and I'm forever stumbling over them. Why, I'm sure she's brought out half a dozen goddaughters at least."

"Yes. She wished to oversee my comeout as well. She wanted me to stay with her, from time to time, long before that. But Papa refused. He—well, he said he didn't believe in that foolishness." She hesitated.

"Foolishness? Oh. I see. Why put you on the Marriage Mart when he already had a husband for you?"

"Well, that was part of it." She felt a tad uncomfortable discussing family affairs with a stranger, even if he was Aunt Clem's nephew.

"And the other part?" he prodded.

"Really, you're the most inquisitive gentleman, Mr. Trevelyan."

"I want to know. I want to know what evil curse has kept us apart all these years."

She turned to look at him again, and he smiled. What a lovely, lazy smile, she thought. It made one feel so peaceful and relaxed, even while one's instincts warned one otherwise.

"No evil curse," she answered. "Only he hated Mama's friends, and has always believed London Society to be shallow, vain, stupid, and vicious. He did agree to a Season when I was eighteen, but until then, Mama lived in London, he was off travelling, and I stayed at our house in the country."

"Ah, I see. He didn't want you to turn out like the rest of Society's debs, so he kept you hidden away from evil influence."

She nodded.

"And what did you do in your rustic haven?"

"I read."

"I see."

Of course he didn't see. How could he? "My governess was rather a bluestocking," she explained. "Consequently, I do not handle my needle very well, and my watercolours are appalling, and—"

"Good heavens! You aren't about to tell me you don't play the pianoforte?"

This being uttered in horrified incredulity, she couldn't help but giggle, even as she admitted she could play *no* instrument—at least, not very well.

"You poor, benighted girl. What *can* you do?"

"I can, as Papa will tell you, talk a blue streak."

"Then talk, by all means, Miss Ashmore. It is, after all, the only *safe* thing one—or two, rather—can do upon a horse."

Deciding it was best to ignore his innuendoes, she invited him to choose a subject.

"Tell me of Albania. Tell me what you've discovered about Byron's 'rugged nurse of savage men.' "

She complied with his request, and he was a little surprised at what she said. She'd read neither Hobhouse's *Travels in Albania* nor Byron's *Childe Harold*, for those books had been published while she was travelling with her father. Thus, her perspective was all her own, with the focus on politics though she drew analogies from both literature and history. It wasn't a typical bluestocking speech—or at least, certainly not like that of any bluestocking he'd ever known. Her turn of mind was interesting, and her voice very pleasant to hear. Her letter, Basil supposed, had promised something, but this was more than he'd hoped for. He thought better of his aunt as a result, and the time passed more quickly than he'd expected, considering that it was not whiled away with dalliance.

They did not, as Basil had predicted, have to ride all night, though he guessed it was well past midnight when they reached the edge of the village to be met by Sir Charles, Mr. Burnham, and the Albanian servants. Alexandra, half-dead from exhaustion, gave herself over to Lefka's care and was lead away to a tiny cottage.

Meanwhile, Basil was set upon by the two Englishmen, who immediately began questioning him. Yes, he told them, Miss Ashmore was quite unharmed. No, he assured them, there would be no more trouble.

"But I must beg your pardon, gentlemen. It has been such an interesting day altogether that I am like to drop from fatigue. I assure you I cannot put another answer together tonight. We will talk more tomorrow. If you would be so kind as to point me in the direction of a comfortable mound of earth—or a stump or a rock—and topple me onto it, I should be very much obliged."

3

THE FOLLOWING MORNING, after being ungently wakened by the faithful Gregor, Basil betook himself to a mountain stream for a rather chilly bath. Then, clean in body—though his travel-stained garments distressed his fastidious soul—he found Sir Charles and took him aside for private conversation.

Having upon awakening become painfully sensible of a fragrance of goat about her person, Alexandra was making her own morning ablutions about the time the two gentlemen were having their chat. Lefka, who stood guard nearby, persisted in making the most indecorous remarks regarding the beautiful young man who'd rescued her charge. As a result, Miss Ashmore was not only ravenously hungry but unrefreshingly hot and flustered by the time she joined the others for breakfast. One look at her father's face told her there was more aggravation to come.

"I'd like to have a word with you, Alexandra," he announced.

"Can't it wait until after breakfast, Papa? I haven't eaten a thing since yesterday morning—"

"Breakfast can wait."

She looked longingly at the table set under the grape arbour: thick slabs of bread, fruit, two kinds of highly aromatic cheese, and thick black coffee. But her father led her inexorably back into the little cottage.

"I've just had a startling conversation with Mr. Trevelyan, Alexandra."

Abruptly, one of Lefka's most lurid suggestions came back to her. She blushed furiously.

"Ah, my dear, your face tells me that it is true. But why did you never confide this thing to your Papa?" His words sounded sorrowful, but the creases were settling into his forehead.

She collected herself, speaking carefully. "Because I couldn't think you'd like it, Papa. He had nothing when I met him, and though I believed in him, I couldn't expect that you would."

"No, and I don't like it now." He then proceeded to remind her at interminable length about obligations, filial devotion, and the superior character of Mr. Burnham.

Since she'd heard all of this several hundred times before, there was no need to attend very closely. Instead, she concentrated on how best to manage her stubborn Papa. When he finally paused for breath, she answered as though she'd considered all he'd said very seriously. "Of course, that's all true, Papa. But you don't know Mr. Trevelyan yet, do you? Hasn't he made something of himself—starting with nothing—in only six years? And hasn't he been true to me all this while? With his background he might have had his pick of brides in England, but instead he's worked and sacrificed—all for me. Even if I did now have some doubt of my feelings—for I was only eighteen when I met him—I must esteem him for his courage and devotion."

This was doing it rather brown—especially the part about being true to her, when she strongly suspected that Mr. Trevelyan had about as much notion of fidelity as a tomcat. Nonetheless, Alexandra would have cheerfully committed any extravagance that promised freedom from the ghastly Burnhams.

Sir Charles, however, was not to be won over so easily. "Yes, dear, I daresay the young man has behaved admirably. But really, what choice had he, if he had, as you say, nothing? And what of Mr. Burnham's patience? He has waited several years, never complaining."

Well, of course he wouldn't complain. He didn't care one way or other about it. Summoning up all her patience, Alexandra dutifully endured her father's anxieties about the Burnhams, who even now must be preparing for the wedding.

"And what of Society?" he persisted. "Everyone knows you're promised to Randolph. No one knows anything of any attachment to Mr. Trevelyan. You'll be labelled 'jilt.' And everyone will think that the Ashmores have no sense of honour."

Bother your honour, Alexandra thought. And to talk of Society—as if he'd ever in his life cared what Society thought about anything, as if anyone in Society had ever heard of the Burnhams—was the height of absurdity.

Squelching a sigh of vexation, she answered ingenuously, "I don't understand, Papa, how it's less dishonourable to abandon a man who's sacrificed so much on my account and trusted me all these years to keep my promise to him."

The baronet was growing exasperated. He couldn't in all honesty claim that she had no obligation to Mr. Trevelyan. Sir Charles was beginning to feel cornered. "This is merely a childish infatuation, Alexandra. As I'm sure you and Mr. Trevelyan will soon find out. People change in six years. What seems romantic at eighteen looks very different at four-and-twenty."

She gazed at him as though struck by what he said. Then, in a slow, thoughtful voice, she answered. "Well, to tell the truth, I hadn't thought of that, Papa. I was so overjoyed to see him again—and as my gallant rescuer. I suppose it was very romantic."

Her father nodded, looking obnoxiously complacent. But his complacency began to fade as she went on.

"In that case, I don't see what you're alarmed about. For if it is, as you say, only infatuation, then we'll discover it soon enough, won't we? Very likely, by the time we're home again—or soon after, surely—Mr. Trevelyan and I will have taken each other in dislike. And everything will settle itself peaceably with neither dishonour nor hurt feelings. How perceptive you are, Papa."

Papa being, as they say, hoist with his own petard, could produce no answer for this. He had to content himself with grumbling about childish infatuations and wondering why he and Randolph should have to put up with such behaviour. However, as it turned out, he hadn't time to annoy himself or his daughter much more on that subject. They'd no sooner left the house and joined the others near the grape arbour when they heard in the distance a dull thundering.

This gradually resolved itself into the pounding of hooves, and then in turn became a lone figure on a brown stallion. The figure came to a halt some yards from where the group now stood, watching in alarm.

"Ah, the rejected swain," Basil murmured, moving quickly to Alexandra's side and putting a protective arm about her shoulders. Though the gesture filled Sir Charles with ineffable disgust, he had sense enough to hold his tongue.

The rejected swain was soon before them, looking so humble and abashed that Alexandra's heart, which had been pounding in concert with the horse's hooves, swiftly settled itself to a mere fluttering.

"Zotir Ashmore," said the young man quietly. "Zotir Tri—Tri—Vasil." He looked at Alexandra and heaved a great sigh. Then, raising himself very tall, very straight, he launched into a long, beautiful—nearly poetic—apology. While it was not nearly so poetic in English, the tone alone impressed his listeners. He had shamed his family and disgraced himself. His behaviour was madness and inexcusable. He despaired of obtaining their forgiveness.

The speech made Alexandra feel ashamed of having deceived him with her make-believe fiancé. Dhimitri was obviously sincere, and now, standing there so tall and sad and dignified, he was, she thought, noble.

Good heavens! now he was saying that he must go with them to Prevesa to make what small amends were in his power. He would personally see to their comfort and safety during their "perilous journey." He had friends and relatives in many of the villages along the way, who would make them all welcome.

"Would you tell him, Alexandra," Basil responded, when Dhimitri's offer had been translated, "that we accept his apology. His offer, however, is too generous. There's no need for him to accompany us."

Zotir Vasil was also generous, but the thing must be done. If Dhimitri could not bring his family assurances that the English had reached their destination safely, he could not go home at all.

It soon was plain that the offer must be accepted.

Sir Charles so counselled Basil in a low-spoken aside. "The boy comes of a good family, Mr. Trevelyan, and they're very proud. He must redeem his honour, and we could use the protection—though I must say it is deuced awkward, under the circumstances."

"Well, then, he must come, I suppose. Alexandra, my love"—she saw her father start at this—"I hope you have not too many other beaux between here and Prevesa. Otherwise, I fear we'll soon swell up into a great army and have Ali Pasha quaking in his slippers by the time we reach our destination."

"You see the difficulty."

"Ay, that I do, my lady." Mr. Henry Latham accepted a cup of tea from his hostess. "Burnham's a very close man with his affairs. My people have learned nothing that isn't plain and aboveboard. The situation may very well be as he says, you know. As the match means a step up in the world for them, it's worth a good deal more than the gold."

"Then you agree it's futile to attempt to communicate with him?" Lady Bertram asked.

"Oh, yes. A waste of pen and ink. And not only on account of this," he added. "George, you see, is preoccupied lately, due to problems with his labourers."

Lady Bertram smiled faintly. "Is he now?"

"Yes. And I expect it's going to get worse before it gets better. As things always do." Mr. Latham expressed this pessimistic opinion with the utmost amiability, as he carried a tea cake to his plate. "It's what comes of not paying an honest day's pay for an honest day's work. Your labouring classes like to get paid fair for what they do. It's a queer thing, but there it is. Human nature, my lady."

"You are a student of human nature, sir," the countess remarked drily.

"In my own modest way."

"Then what do you make of the other matter?"

Mr. Latham made it out, apparently, while he disposed of the tea cake. After it had vanished into the depths of his plump, genial countenance, he answered, "It's one thing to study human nature and another to predict it. I'm a businessman, not a prophet. But as a businessman—" He paused.

"I'm always eager to hear your views on business, sir."

"Well, then, as a man of business I can give you a fair idea of what ships are scheduled to cross the Mediterranean. Always allowing, of course, for the complications of this unfortunate unpleasantness on the continent. With good information and a little patience, I expect we can manage to be on the spot when that particular ship comes in."

"The information I leave, as always, to you. As to patience—only point me to the port, Henry, and I shall wait there, patiently as Job, though it take a twelvemonth."

Was it not enough that he'd done three years' penance in vile climates among villains whose treacheries made his own attempted "crime" a mere boyish prank by comparison? Was it not enough he'd been nearly murdered some dozen times? Apparently, the Furies were not done tormenting him. He must now spend all his waking hours with one of the most desirable women he'd ever met—and have to keep his hands to himself the whole blessed time.

The Devil himself must have fashioned her to make men demented. Small wonder that Dhimitri, perceiving Mr. Burnham's profound and incomprehensible want of interest, had tried to carry her off. Even the jaded Mr. Trevelyan would like to carry her off to some private place.

The Devil, surely, had designed her long-legged slenderness, so exquisitely curved, and woven her dark chestnut curls to glint copper in the bright sun. He'd sculpted the soft, full lips; and then, for Old Nick hadn't any conscience at all, he'd drawn those startling green eyes with their flecks of gold like speckled sunlight in a cool forest. Nor was that yet enough. She must move with sensuous, provocative grace and speak in that husky, intimate timbre. Even her unfashionably tanned skin must seem the palest golden silk, rising to a warm rose in her cheeks. All that, and Basil could do no more than look.

For one, she was the daughter of a gentleman. For another, she was obviously innocent; and for a third—and this carried by far the greatest weight—she was Aunt Clem's goddaughter. He wouldn't even have to compromise Miss Ashmore to be forced into marriage. She had only to become infatuated with him and confide it to Aunt Clem, and his bachelor days would be over. He needed to repeat this lecture to himself often as the days passed, for she made him very . . . restless.

Basil was not used to resisting temptation of any kind. When in his life had he lusted in vain? But then, when had he ever lusted after a gently bred virgin? Never. His problem was simply that he'd been too long without feminine companionship and wasn't used to controlling himself.

Still, they must keep up a show for the Argus-eyed

Dhimitri. Therefore, Mr. Trevelyan was forced to sit very close to Miss Ashmore when they ate their modest meals. He must, certainly, engage her in conversation, though it only made him more restless. The more he talked to her, the more he wanted to talk to her.

It was partly because she was well educated and articulate. But there was something else, too, something he couldn't quite put his finger on. More than once he'd heard her render her intellectual Papa speechless with frustration after one of her exercises in twisted logic. What truly surprised Basil, however, was that he found himself, more often than he liked, at *point non plus*.

Though he didn't mean to flirt with her and knew it was dangerous, sometimes he'd forget about Aunt Clem and the life of idle dissipation awaiting him in England. He'd lapse into his coaxing ways, and she'd seem to respond as sweetly as he wished—until he realised that her tender glances and soft words were a precise imitation of his own. Every time, instead of taking offence, he'd end up laughing at himself and, in the next minute, making the most candid confessions.

Afterwards, when he thought about it, he felt uneasy. He wasn't used to being managed and objected to it on principle. Yet while it was happening it was, well, so *refreshing*. Anyhow, he reassured himself, it was a good idea to be candid with her. Knowing what he was, she'd be intelligent enough to keep on her guard against him.

Though it was only about forty miles or so from Gjirokastra to Saranda, the poor roads made it a journey of several days. As the time passed, Sir Charles grew more and more frustrated. The infatuation showed no signs of diminishing. On the contrary, his daughter and Trevelyan had too much to say to each other. They talked constantly, starting at breakfast and not leaving off until they retired for the night. Sir Charles would have preferred to keep them apart, but with Dhimitri present he didn't dare. Even

Gjergi, who had spoken with the rejected swain at length, warned the baronet. Dhimitri had given the girl up only because he was convinced that she and Vasil were fated to be together. It was *kismet*.

Kismet, indeed. Well, they were a pair, those two, with their glib answers to everything. It would serve them right to be shackled to each other for the rest of their days. Looking now at Randolph—who rode along calmly, quite oblivious to the various tensions and countertensions of the party—the baronet remembered the debt he owed and decided to drop his assistant a hint.

In response, the conscientious Mr. Burnham, who'd rarely troubled to say more than two words a day to Miss Ashmore, began obediently to seek her out for conversation.

On the third afternoon of their journey, Mr. Trevelyan remarked to Miss Ashmore on this strange development as they sat, a little apart from the others, eating grapes.

She chuckled at this, and said, "He's courting me, Mr. Trevelyan. Can't you see? Papa must have told him to do it—and probably has hinted what to say, as well."

"You laugh, Miss Ashmore? I'm shocked. Still, with three men breaking their hearts over you, what else would a cruel girl like yourself do?"

"Three hearts? But you told me only yesterday you hadn't any heart at all."

"I never said any such thing."

"You implied it when you spoke of Almacks."

"I said only that I was looking forward to the experience."

"Yes, but you said it in such a self-satisfied way that I knew you were picturing all the lovely young ladies wanting you to notice them."

"You make me sound a perfect coxcomb. What a cruel construction to put on my innocent remarks."

"Then you mustn't let your eyes glitter so wickedly

when you speak of such things, Mr. Trevelyan. I can quite read your mind."

For half an instant, he believed she could. He went on amiably to insist he *did* have a heart. "True, it's very small and very hard. Nonetheless, it exists and may, therefore, be broken."

"Well, I wish you wouldn't break it just yet, or between that and the other two you tease me of, we shall leave a deal of rubble behind us."

"Point taken, Miss Ashmore. I shall refrain from littering this lovely landscape. Still, I do worry that Mr. Burnham will steal you out from under my nose."

"Do you worry, poor man? But you're young and resilient. I daresay you could reconcile yourself to the loss quickly enough."

He immediately looked such a picture of wounded innocence that she nearly choked on the grape she'd popped into her mouth. She looked at him in wonder. "I declare you were meant for the stage. However do you manage those expressions?"

"Practice, my dear," he answered, with an odd little smile. "Practice."

According to Mr. Burnham, who was dutifully, if not altogether effectively, attempting to distract Alexandra from her Other Fiancé, Mr. Trevelyan also had considerable practice in deceit.

As they left Delvina and began their descent to the plain of Vurqu, Randolph had—in the politest way—replaced his rival at Miss Ashmore's side. A tad annoyed to see Basil give way so easily and go on so amicably to join her Papa—with whom he was now engaged in lively conversation—Alexandra gave Mr. Burnham a dazzling smile and asked him what he meant.

He was not in the habit of eliciting warm acknowledgement from Miss Ashmore. When she regarded him at all, and when he noticed, both of which were rare happenings, she did so mainly with profound weariness. So taken aback was he by this display of warmth that he smiled automatically in return.

It occurred to Alexandra that he wasn't a bad-looking man. Randolph's clear blue eyes, when not glazed over in their customary scholarly abstraction, were, at least, honest ones. You could believe what you saw there.

"I only hope he will not deceive *you*," said Randolph, coloring slightly.

"What makes you think he will, Randolph? I thought you'd never met him before."

He hesitated briefly, then admitted that he hadn't.

"Then to what do you ascribe your concern?"

"I shouldn't have brought it up. I'd rather not speak ill of a man behind his back."

Well then, Alexandra thought, glancing at Mr. Trevelyan, who seemed to find Papa inordinately amusing today, let us by all means call him to us so you can speak ill to his face.

Aloud she said, "It isn't kind to drop such alarming hints to me, Randolph, and then say nothing more. Surely you must have some basis for what you claim."

As a scholar who prided himself on his logic, Mr. Burnham wasn't about to own he had no foundation for his remarks. On the other hand, it went against his gentlemanly grain to trade in gossip. The scholar won out.

"I was in London some two years after you left, as you know. While we did not travel in the same circles, I did hear of Mr. Trevelyan, and, I'm sorry to say, nothing to his credit. When I heard this story of six years' trying to make his fortune, I was astonished. Knowing what I did, I could not imagine that he had got his money any other way than by gambling."

Well, this was of a piece with everything else—and surely Randolph wouldn't say such a thing if he didn't have reasonable evidence. Gambling, too. Add that to the rest and it made a pretty sort of blackguard.

What of it, then? She certainly wasn't going to marry the fellow. Fortified by this comforting certainty, she rose—as she must—to Mr. Trevelyan's defence. "That would be very distressing news, indeed. But he *was* in low spirits when I last saw him," she lied, "and I understand that some men will turn to vice—temporarily—when they're in low spirits. Besides, he does say he's partners with Henry Latham, and we could always find out the truth of that."

Randolph nodded gravely. "Mr. Latham is a distant acquaintance of my father. It won't be difficult to ascertain the facts once we are home. Perhaps I wrong the man. I don't mean to. It is only that I cannot like to see you misled."

He was sincere, of course. Honest as the day is long: that was Randolph. He made her feel guilty. A little while in Mr. Trevelyan's company and she'd deceived her father, Randolph, and even Dhimitri. But when men persisted in being such blockheads, what else could one do? Still, maybe she'd been overhasty in rejecting Randolph. Charm and clever conversation weren't everything. Better to be a little bored occasionally than to be forever worrying what one's untrustworthy spouse might be up to.

Dear heavens! Whatever had led her into that train of thought? What unworthy spouse could she possibly be thinking of?

Randolph was still making apologetic murmurs. Alexandra collected her wandering thoughts and made him a soothing reply—exactly the sort of thing his wife would have to say every now and then when some bit of stone puzzled him or when he lost one of his sketches. Well, he was kind and sincere, but there were other men in the world. Nothing on earth—except perhaps her stubborn father—obliged her to choose between these two alone. Not that they were, she chided herself, willing to be chosen from. Had not one of them made that very clear the first night she met him?

4

SARANDA NOW BORE few traces of its origins as the ancient, thriving seaport of Onchesmus. It was a port, still, but a very minor one, and so a boat must be hired to take the group on to Prevesa. With luck—ill luck, as Alexandra saw it—they might speedily obtain places on one of the British vessels that regularly stopped there.

There was news in Saranda of Napoleon and contradictory tales of a great battle in France or Belgium. The outcome of that battle, unfortunately, was a matter of violent debate.

Basil was standing with Miss Ashmore, waiting for the dragomen to finish bullying the townsfolk as they loaded their belongings into the tiny boat.

"I suppose," he said, "we must wait until we get to Prevesa—or even Malta—to learn for certain. I should like to know, in the first place, how the Corsican eluded the British cruisers guarding his island. Then I should be curious to find out why he didn't attack Wellington in Brussels. He was still in Paris, last I heard—though it was all rumour and everyone contradicting everyone else, just as they do now. I couldn't stop to wait for news." He glanced at his companion.

Miss Ashmore seemed lost in reverie. She was gazing out across the narrow neck of the Ionian Sea towards the gloomy mass of Corfu's mountains.

"What do *you* think will be the outcome?" he asked.

She brought herself back, but her green eyes were still

rather dreamy. "How difficult it is to contemplate war when one gazes upon such peaceful beauty. Yet this has never been a peaceful place. Ali Pasha and his soldiers have conquered, town by town, towns which had been conquered by others before. In time, someone will wrest his dominions from Ali. And he is so much more clever and efficient a manager than Buonaparte," she added, her eyes gleaming now with mischief.

"More Machiavellian, you mean?"

"Certainly that. Ali, I think, would never have been so careless as to alienate Talleyrand. Or if he had, he would have known enough to have the man killed, instead of leaving him to lick his wounds and plot revenge for five long years."

He wondered once again, looking into that heartbreakingly beautiful face, how she came by her opinions. As the daughter of Sir Charles Ashmore, she could hardly be expected to escape without some smattering of historical knowledge. But the baronet knew nothing of current events—beyond the dim awareness that there had been a war going on which occasionally interfered with his travel plans—and she seemed to know everything.

Much of Miss Ashmore's information, Basil had learned, came from divers diplomats the Ashmores had encountered in their travels, especially the many foreigners who paid court to Ali Pasha hoping to lure the sly Albanian to their side. Nonetheless, what Alexandra made of the facts and rumours she heard was her own and always interesting. To egg her on, therefore, he asked ingenuously what she meant. After all, Buonaparte couldn't help but alienate somebody and could hardly trouble himself about whose feelings he might hurt.

She shot him a look of incredulity. "To call the man a stockingful of excrement—and that before the whole court? He could not have helped that? And he reputed a brilliant strategist?"

Basil suppressed a grin. "Called him what?"

But she was already caught up in the drama of the moment she pictured. "Before the whole court," she repeated, shaking her head. "Talleyrand stood and bore the abuse, never saying a word. Yet, one suspects, from that day forth he must have plotted his revenge. Plotted, planned, biding his time for years." She shivered. "Such patience is frightening. I should not care to have such a one about. I imagined him like Cassius, with his 'lean and hungry look.'"

Basil gave his own theatrical shudder. "That sounds exactly like Rogers, my valet. Left to his devices in Prevesa, heaven knows what he might be plotting. I hope, at least, he's guarding my trunks."

"If he's a proper British valet, Mr. Trevelyan, he'll be obliged to shoot himself as soon as he claps eyes on you."

Basil glanced down ruefully at his raffish attire: Turkish-style trousers, limp cotton shirt the Albanians called a *kamisha*, and travel-stained cloak. "Well, you see, my costume doesn't look like anything in particular, and so I can't be categorised, which makes men careful how they treat me. I may, you know, be mad."

Miss Ashmore assured him, with a little grin, of her certainty that he *was*.

"But sane enough to hope Rogers has kept my baggage safe from these rogues. I don't know why he shouldn't, as he's a worse rogue than any of them. At any rate, he'll not deign to notice my disgraceful appearance. He'll take me immediately in hand, and the next time you see me you won't recognise me."

"Ah, then I shan't be obliged to speak to you."

"In which case, I shall travel as I am," was the prompt retort. "But here we are, speaking of my sartorial tragedies, when I am on pins and needles to hear about this Cassius-Talleyrand of yours. And of Napoleon's Fatal Flaw. Is he a tragic figure, do you think?"

It wanted very little to coax her to talk. She led Basil on back through history, from Buonaparte and Talleyrand to

Caesar to Alexander to Alexander's father, Philip of Macedon. Basil was content to go where she led, though he teased and questioned and tried to undermine her theories. He liked to listen to her, liked exploring with her the characters of those who'd made history, and those who'd made art and literature of history.

What had Dhimitri's relatives called her? The English witch. She wove spells, they claimed, entrapping young men with her beauty, but to Basil she was Sheherazade. He could have listened to her forever . . . and oh, how he wished she could keep him company through his long, restless nights.

They reached Prevesa by late afternoon—too soon—and he was jolted out of his trance as they prepared to disembark. Deaf to her protests and oblivious to Dhimitri's congratulatory smile, Basil lifted her out of the boat and waded to shore with her in his arms. No, he thought, he was under no spell. He only liked to hear her talk because he wanted her, and he wanted her because he'd been lonely too many months. There was no spell. Only Desire, and that must fade once they were home.

Lefka, Gjergi, and Stefan had stayed behind in Saranda, but Gregor and Dhimitri refused to part from their charges until those fragile English creatures were safely aboard their ship. A British merchant vessel lay in the harbour, awaiting the escort of a brig of war which was scheduled to arrive the next day and depart the day following.

While Mr. Trevelyan made arrangements for passage, Dhimitri saw to accommodations. The young Albanian had distant relatives in the town who were very well-to-do. Their spacious and well-furnished home was, he insisted, infinitely preferable to the Spartan lodgings of the English vice-consul. Too tired to argue, the travellers agreed to accept the hospitality.

After dinner, their hosts proposed that the Englishmen take a stroll through the town. Alexandra helped the womenfolk wash the simple dinner utensils and then decided to take her own quiet walk through the garden. She had, after all, a great deal to think about.

This make-believe betrothal to Mr. Trevelyan was not a satisfactory solution to her problems. They could not continue the charade after they reached England, which meant she was only postponing the inevitable. Her rakish co-conspirator would no doubt wish to recommence his raking immediately, thereby leaving no more stumbling blocks in Papa's—or rather, the Burnhams'—way. Mr. Trevelyan had turned out to be hardly any help at all, and he unsettled her. She was not used to being unsettled, and she didn't like it. Well, actually, she *did* like it—and that, considering the man's character, was not a desirable state of mind.

Shrugging to shake off her thoughts of him she turned into the pathway leading to the terraced garden, lush with flowers. The air was sweet, but not cloyingly so. The sea breezes stirred and freshened, making it as deliciously fragrant, she thought, as the Garden of Eden must have been. From the distance came strains of the music she'd gradually come to appreciate, though it had sounded so odd and discordant at first. A tenor voice sang in a familiar, aching minor key accompanied by the wail of what sounded like an Eastern version of a clarinet. She couldn't make out the words, but imagined what they were: a tribute to native warriors and patriots or to the rugged beauty of the country. Sometimes there was a mournful song of love—but then, they all sounded rather mournful, even the triumphant tale of Ali Pasha's conquest of Prevesa. As she stopped to listen, she realised she wasn't alone.

Basil stepped away from the garden wall he'd been lounging against, and approached her. He was dressed now, as he'd promised, like a proper English gentleman, though he still seemed somehow a creature of her imagination. In the moonlight his sun-bleached hair was shot through with silver. Even his amber cat eyes seemed to glow as they settled on her in that watchful way.

"I was right," he said, in a low voice. "I was thinking this was almost—but not quite heaven. Now you are come to make it complete."

The words made her heart flutter, as they doubtless were intended to do, but she was determined not to blush. Nor would she be alarmed in the least at the way he so self-assuredly offered his arm. She'd stroll with him for a minute or two and then go back indoors.

"It is beautiful," she answered, deciding the honeyed words were best ignored. "For the six years we've been here, I find myself in one place after another, each time thinking it must be the loveliest scene in the world."

"I suppose then, you'll be sorry to leave?"

"Yes, of course. What other sea is as blue as the Ionian?"

"None. But I shall be deliriously happy to go home, nonetheless."

"You'd have been gone all the sooner if it hadn't been for me," she found herself saying, though that wasn't what she'd meant to say at all.

"Yes, but I wouldn't have been returning *with* you—and that, I think, more than makes up for the delay."

Naturally he'd say something like that. He probably thought she was fishing for compliments.

When she didn't answer, he went on. "Now, of course, all the advantage is with the later departure. Not only do I return with you, but I have managed by sheer perseverance to find you alone at last. It did take some doing, and I was wretchedly deceitful. However, I have my reward, and that's all that matters."

She stopped and looked at him. "What are you doing here, Mr. Trevelyan? I thought you'd gone with my father and Mr. Burnham and the others."

"Why do you never call me Basil? Is the name so disagreeable?"

"That wasn't what I asked, Mr. Trevelyan."

"But it was what *I* asked, Miss Ashmore, and I wish you would stop calling me Mr. Trevelyan. It puts such a monstrous distance between us and makes Dhimitri pity me, which is quite unbearable."

"You keep turning the subject, and yet you were the one to start it."

"Of course I did, and for nothing but the sheer delight of watching your green eyes flash at me. They are indeed flashing, Miss Ashmore, as they always do when I provoke you, and that should make me feel ashamed of myself if anything could. But nothing does, you know."

That was easy enough to believe. "In which case, sir, I think it best to take my leave of you."

She disengaged her arm from his and started to turn back to the house, but he stepped in front of her, blocking the way. He stood only a few inches from her. He was only teasing, of course. He was trying to make her nervous. He was succeeding. "You stand in my path, Mr. Trevelyan, which is very inconsiderate, because now I'll be obliged to trample on that lovely flowerbed."

"I only wanted to kiss you," was the outrageous reply. "Here we are alone in paradise—the perfect moment—and you talk only of murdering these innocent plants."

She was alarmed now, though something pleasantly anticipatory about that alarm brought warmth to her cheeks. He hadn't budged, and the glitter in those strange eyes forced her to look away.

She took a step backward. "I don't know what you're thinking of. What point is there in kissing me when there's no one nearby who needs to be convinced of our undying devotion?" She took another step away from him. He stayed where he was, looking thoughtful.

"How logical you are. I think it's from spending too much time with Mr. Burnham. Randolph. You do call him Randolph. I've heard you. No use denying it."

That was better. His tone was lighter now, and so hers

became. "I've known him for years. But if it troubles you so much, then I'll call you Randolph, too."

Her small grin made him even more restless than usual—or maybe reckless was more accurate a description, because in the very next moment he reached out and pulled her to him. He bent his face to hers, and then there was nothing left but to kiss her. He told himself it was that grin, provoking him.

Miss Ashmore certainly had not meant to let him kiss her in the first place or to kiss him back in the second. But his mouth was so unexpectedly gentle as it touched hers that it gentled her own response. Then there was a warmth, and it was so welcoming and tender and made her feel so very peaceful and cozy and safe in his arms, that she did respond. He'd pulled her closer until her heart was pounding, and the press of his lean, muscular body had kindled warmth into blazing heat, and everything familiar had been whirled away by the maelstrom into which he drew her.

She was, suddenly, very afraid of him, because he was drawing her into danger, and she was following too willingly. His fingers were in her hair. He kissed her forehead and her eyelids and her cheeks, and when his lips found her mouth again they were hungry, demanding, urgent. Because she did not want him to stop, tears—of frustration, anger, shame, she hardly knew—welled up in her eyes as she tried to push him away.

"No," he whispered, crushing her closer. "Not now."

"Yes, stop. Now," she gasped. "Please stop—you must stop. Please."

He barely seemed to notice her effort to push him away. "Alexandra." His voice was hoarse.

"Let go of me."

Very unwillingly he released her from his embrace, but he clasped her hand to keep her from fleeing. "This is a terrible time to stop, my love," he told her. He sounded rather breathless as though he'd been running hard.

"Oh, please. No 'my loves.' And will you let go of me? I must go back."

"You can't do that now, Alexandra. Look at you. Your wicked fiancé has disarranged your hair, and your eyes are wet. You look exactly as though—well, exactly as you should under the circumstances." Releasing her, he offered his handkerchief. "And you hate me, which is a great deal worse."

She dabbed absently at her eyes but made no other effort to restore herself to rights. Stunned and confused, she spoke without thinking. "It isn't that . . . I don't know what it is. I don't understand."

At the moment, there were a few things he didn't understand either. There was, for instance, the totally ungovernable desire. If she hadn't begged him to stop in that desperate voice, he wasn't sure what would have happened. Surely it must have stopped at some point. He refused to think beyond that.

She wasn't looking at him, but was staring off into the dark distance, as though some secret might be stored there. Somewhere in that distance there was music: a mournful, lonely voice calling to the heavens. Her face was like cool marble in the moonlight, so still did she stand, gazing off at nothing. He wanted to touch her, to make her warm again and yielding as she had been—but no, that was quite impossible. Firmly, he turned his mind away and became more charming. "I do hope you'll settle on hating yourself then, because you'll be kinder to me, and I do need a great deal of kindness now after being so cruelly rejected."

"Rejected?" She looked up in astonishment at those strange cat eyes, but they were blank and innocent.

"Isn't that what it was? 'No' and 'stop' to me mean rejection, especially when uttered in such anguish. Yet you needn't expect me to apologise. I'd gladly do the same again, even to be rejected again though that isn't the least bit pleasant, and you may certainly apologise if you like. I'm a very forgiving sort of person, you know."

Good heavens, but he was impossible. To chatter at her so when she was racked by emotions she could neither understand nor name. She stared at him. He stared back, his face still blank and innocent, as the silence lengthened between them. It was not a peaceful sort of silence. Something seemed to vibrate within it. That something finally drove Alexandra to regain her self-command and make a rather tart comment on his magnanimity.

"Yes, magnanimity is one of my failings. But come," he went on briskly, "your current state of dishevelment is unconscionably tempting, and I don't think I can contemplate you another minute without doing something perfectly dreadful."

Thus admonished, she attended to her hair—as best she could, with his helpful interference. He insisted the pins were in wrong and, looking very grave, pulled them out almost as quickly as she put them in. His touch, as he handed them back to her, made her tremble.

"Will you please stop helping me?" she snapped. "I'll be out here all night at this rate."

"You didn't think I intended to let you go back in so soon? However tedious my company seems to you, we've been here only a very few minutes."

"That's quite long enough to be alone in a dark garden with a gentleman, even in Albania. It's hardly proper."

"No, it isn't proper at all, and if I could think of some beautiful lie to convince you to stay—well, obviously, you can't trust me to behave myself."

"That's true. And it's very tiresome and unfair of you, Mr. Trevelyan—"

"Mr. Trevelyan, still."

"Randolph, then."

"Basil, you wretched girl. *Basil.*"

"Basil, then." Seeing the triumphant smile he wore, she smiled, too. He might have all the experience, but he needn't always have the upper hand. "Basil then, my love, my sweet," she went on in falsely ardent, breathless tones so like his own that she startled the smile off his face. "You are monstrous unfair. For you show me not only that I'm not safe in your company, but that you're unsafe in mine. I must look out not only for myself, but for you as well—since you seem bound and determined to compromise me."

"Do I?" he asked. He made no move to stop her when she stepped away. His smile was gone, and the bland innocence had turned to watchfulness again.

"Oh, yes. But I gave you my promise, and I mean to keep it, regardless how difficult you make it for me. I will save you from yourself, Basil, my love. So rest easy."

She turned then and left him.

=5=

ALTHOUGH SHE FOUND the voyage unspeakably tedious, Alexandra inwardly cursed the favourable winds that sped them on to England and the Burnhams. They learned along the way that the defeated Buonaparte had preceded them and, even now, was being ogled by curious mobs at Tor Bay. Their own vessel's captain, however, had no interest in twice-vanquished Corsicans and, furthermore, was in a tremendous hurry. He made directly for Portsmouth. There they were amazed to find both Henry Latham and Lady Bertram waiting for them, and in very short order these two contrived to separate Alexandra from her father.

Papa, it is true, did not leave his daughter willingly, but Lady Bertram swept all his objections away as though they were so many odd bits of scrap in her path.

"To Yorkshire?" she repeated, in magnificently disdainful, disbelieving tones. "At this time of year and after so arduous a journey? Unthinkable, my dear boy. I fear you must be near collapse yourself to harbour such a notion." To his stunned protests she answered severely, "You have cheated me of her company for six long years—and after dear Juliet had promised me I might give the girl a Season." This, of course, was a monstrous fib, but Papa didn't know that.

When he attempted to explain about betrothals and impatient Burnhams, Lady Bertram only gazed coldly down her patrician nose at him and demanded *what* he was thinking of to subject his daughter to the scandal that must arise if she were married so soon upon her return and in such a havey-cavey way.

Sir Charles was not easily cowed, but he was operating under certain disadvantages. He did not like being cast as the villain of the piece, especially when his solution was so reasonable. At once it settled both his debt to the Burnhams and the matter of finding his troublesome daughter a steady husband. Furthermore, there was nothing wrong with Randolph. His character was blameless, he was comfortably well-off, and he was good-looking enough to please any number of romantic females. If Alexandra would only cooperate, her father would not have to waste time dawdling in England when there was so much to be done in Albania. Still, Sir Charles considered himself a just man, and there was this business of Mr. Trevelyan's six years' toil. The tale appeared to be a great piece of nonsense concocted by his scheming daughter and Clementina's nephew, and yet it might be true.

Therefore, though he resented Lady Bertram's high-handed ways and mistrusted his daughter, he was somewhat relieved to have the problem taken off his hands temporarily. He'd like to have the leisure to think things over without being influenced by either Alexandra's sophistries or Mr. Trevelyan's treacly blandishments. To save face, however, he goaded Lady Bertram into delivering a few more ominous predictions and biting comments before giving himself up to be led away by the affable Mr. Latham.

Basil was led away as well, along with Randolph. Alexandra had time only to bid a hasty farewell to her two fiancés and kiss her father's cheek before she was whirled off in the countess's luxurious carriage.

"Well," the great lady said, "that went a deal easier than I expected. Your father was rather more fuddled than usual—I expect that accounts for his not being so obstinate as usual. I was anticipating quite a battle. What, I wonder, accounts for his fuddlement?"

"I think you have your nephew to thank for that, my lady."

"Aunt Clem, if you please. You never used to be so formal, Alexandra. Or is the wretched boy to blame for that, as well?"

The scrutiny of those sharp, brown eyes was a trifle disconcerting. Lady Bertram had such a way of ferreting out secrets—almost as if she read your mind—and Alexandra did not like to have her mind read. Still, she made herself meet that gaze directly and answered, "No, that's my own doing. You were so majestic back there that I'm in awe of you myself."

"Well, your father is not easily awed normally. But tell me, how did Basil unsettle him so?"

Alexandra gave her a slightly abbreviated account of their make-believe romance. Actually, it was only abbreviated in two particulars, for though it was very easy to confide in dear Aunt Clem, one must draw the line at discussing her nephew's embraces. Broad-minded as the countess was, she might think Alexandra compromised, and that would never do.

Lady Bertram found the recitation highly amusing. "Leave it to Basil to find excuses for kissing a pretty gel."

"Oh, but he never—"

"Well, if he never then it most certainly cannot be my nephew we speak of. He is not in the habit of exerting himself on anyone else's account without making it as agreeable to himself as possible. I am disappointed, however, he could contrive no better scheme. It is not at all what I'd hoped for. Still, I daresay he found it immensely entertaining." Her tone, softened. "I hope he did not misbehave terribly, my dear."

Alexandra coloured slightly, though she replied calmly enough. "Oh no, of course not. It was all for show. He did have my father to convince and Dhimitri as well—at least until we were aboard ship. He was very successful. As you saw yourself, Papa was rather confused. The only push he made was to tell Randolph to stir himself."

"Nevertheless, in your father's eyes you're still betrothed to Randolph. It really makes me wonder at Basil."

"You speak as though he regularly accomplishes miracles, Aunt Clem."

"I know he's solved far more difficult and delicate matters for the Crown. It is usually a matter of pride with him to succeed completely at what he undertakes, particularly if it is something devious."

"Perhaps, then, the problem was beneath him."

"That would be a first," the countess muttered.

"Besides, Papa was suspicious of him. Add that to the problem of paying back Mr. Burnham. He did fund Papa's work generously and had those travel accounts published. He looks after all Papa's business now—though there's little enough profit in it for him."

"Yes, a philanthropist, I'm sure," was the dry observation. "How warm you are in defence of your tormentors, Alexandra."

"I've been trying to see it through Papa's eyes, Aunt Clem. After all, I've made so many difficulties for him. And I honestly wish I could care more for Randolph."

The fervour with which she expressed that wish made Lady Bertram raise an eyebrow ever so slightly, but lost in her own thoughts, Alexandra continued, "Papa says I'm only being obstinate—and maybe he's right."

The eyebrow elevated another fraction.

"After all," the young woman went on hurriedly, "Randolph is a kind and honest man. One could do a great deal worse, I suppose."

"Undoubtedly."

"Once he began taking the trouble to talk with me, I found him, well, not disagreeable company. He was most considerate throughout the voyage, certainly, and he *is* sincere and straightforward. One never wonders what he means, really—" She caught herself up in time and went on more matter-of-factly, "At any rate, I think better of him now than when I wrote you. Yet, if I hadn't written and your nephew hadn't come and shaken Randolph out of his complacency, I might never have seen his—Randolph's—better qualities."

Though the words were rational enough, there was an edge of despair in the tone. Nonetheless, Lady Bertram only nodded and remarked, "Basil comes out of the adventure quite a prodigy of virtue. How very distressing that must be for him, after devoting so much time and imagination to wickedness."

"Has he?" Alexandra couldn't help asking. "I mean, has he always been wicked?"

"My dear child—you don't mean to tell me he's pulled the wool over your eyes?"

"Of course not. I was only wondering if he was always so."

The countess hesitated, but only for a moment. Then, without mincing matters—yet without dwelling on them either—she gave her goddaughter a concise history of Basil's career from the time he entered Oxford.

When she had done, Miss Ashmore nodded as though the account was only confirmation of what she'd known all along. She smiled, very winningly indeed, and asked for news of Family and Society—in short, all the sorts of things a young lady who'd been out of England for six years would want to know.

A week later, as Alexandra reclined upon a chaise longue trying to read a book, she found herself wondering where Basil was and what wickedness he could be up to now. *Sense and Sensibility* lay neglected on her lap while she debated whether his new ladybird was an actress or an opera dancer and whether her eyes were blue or brown or even green like Alexandra's own.

But what concern was that of hers? She hadn't really expected him to visit her, had she? Still, she'd thought he might at least call on his own aunt. The days had passed, and there was no sign of him. Doubtless he was too busy with his dissipations.

She was a fool to wait and brood like Miss Austen's painfully passionate Marianne, pining in vain for her faithless Willoughby. At any rate, there were far better things in store for Alexandra Ashmore. Tonight she would dine with the Deverells and meet a young gentleman who'd been invited especially on her account.

"Randolph is all well and good, my dear," Lady Bertram had told her. "If you come to have a care for him, so much the better as you'll please yourself and your father all at once. But I'd rather you looked around a bit first. Marriage is usually a permanent arrangement, you know."

Tonight it was proposed that Alexandra look at one William Farrington, Marquess of Arden, heir to the Duke of Thorne, and "as handsome a devil as you're like to meet," according to Aunt Clem.

"He's all on pins and needles to meet you, my dear. He caught a glimpse of you the other afternoon as you left Madame Vernisse's and pestered Maria day and night for an introduction."

Alexandra closed Miss Austen's book with a resigned thump. Well then, she'd look at him, and he'd look at her. It would be pleasant if he was handsome and even more pleasant if he was also relatively intelligent—though that might be too much to hope for. Her experience of idle, upper-class English gentlemen had led her to conclude that they were exemplars of the evils of inbreeding and, in short, not very bright.

Mr. Trevelyan was bright, however. He did listen, too, and his answers were never patronising even if he did tease dreadfully. She missed his teasing, missed looking for the reality in his theatrical effusions and the bit of truth in his charming lies, just as much as she missed for once being treated by a man as an intellectual equal.

There had even been those rare occasions when she'd

startled him out of his formidable composure. She'd certainly surprised him that last night in Prevesa. Apparently, he'd taken her words to heart, for he'd been scrupulously well behaved through the whole voyage. She didn't like to admit it, but she wished he'd been a little less well behaved.

That was the problem. She might have reasonably pleasant thoughts about him, except that the memory of his embrace kept intruding. Perhaps it wasn't terrible to enjoy being kissed—not when one was kissed so beautifully by so experienced a gentleman. With all that experience to inform it, perhaps a kiss *should* be enjoyable. Practice does make perfect after all. Still, the heat and breathlessness and sudden, frightening urgency of it—well, *that* wasn't proper. No, that part could not be proper.

Which was, of course, why respectable young women did not go off alone with gentlemen and get themselves kissed. What started as a lovely kiss was bound to turn into something else, something that led to ruination.

It was humiliating to admit even to herself that she'd been—at least at the moment—willing to risk such ruin. She flushed at the memory. Pride, not regard for her virtue, had stopped her. She was afraid they'd be caught and forced to wed. Yes, Mr. Trevelyan did make her think wicked thoughts, and yes, he was very attractive, and yes, his kisses were lovely. But as a husband—one who'd resent and hate her for entrapping him, who'd humiliate her with his mistresses—he was out of the question.

How careless of him to begin it in the first place, to think only of amusing himself, and leave her to worry about the consequences. But why not? Hadn't she behaved like a common lightskirt? What was wrong with her anyhow? Was she wicked? Was she infatuated with him? Or was it only that he was so skilled a seducer?

Yes, that must be it. She was the innocent victim of his wiles.

While the innocent victim of Basil Trevelyan's wiles was staring obliviously at Miss Austen's book, Mr. Trevelyan himself had been having a highly agreeable conversation with Mr. Weston of Bond Street. Basil was just finishing his business with the tailor when Lord Arden sauntered in.

The marquess's enthusiastic greeting caused Basil to look at him suspiciously. While their families were intimate, and the two young men had grown up together and caroused and gambled together, they were rather too much alike to trust each other overmuch. Thus, no real intimacy had evolved between them despite many opportunities.

In a very few minutes, the mystery was solved. "I say, Trev," Lord Arden drawled as they left the tailor's shop and made their way to Watier's, "who is that perfectly stunning creature your aunt's taken in?"

Only a week and she'd called herself to Arden's attention. Naturally. Every rogue remaining in London must have sensed her presence in their midst, just as experienced hounds would sniff out a fox. Basil pretended to think very hard.

"Stunning creature?" he asked ingenuously.

"Why, you sly devil. Of course you know who I mean— is this some sort of family secret? Your aunt refuses to be at home to me, and Maria won't say a word, only tells me I might come to dinner tonight and perhaps the young lady will be there. You must tell me who the mysterious beauty is."

"If Lady Deverell is determined to tease you, then I certainly won't spoil her fun." To dinner. What the deuce did the woman mean by inviting one of London's most notorious rakeshames to dinner with Miss Ashmore? Arden's reputation was worse even than Basil's. The marquess had both enormous wealth and exalted rank and took full advantage of the privileges attached thereunto.

Not, certainly, that Basil could have expected an invitation. Lord Deverell, Isabella's father, was hardly likely to welcome into his home the young man who'd threatened his wife's reputation and his daughter's future.

"Then you *do* know," Lord Arden said, calling Basil back to the present. "Well, I must be content to look upon it as a delicious mystery. Obviously, I dare not describe her to anyone and invite rivals. Not, of course, that there's anyone in town at this time of year. Still, I expect she will be there tonight. Maria can't be as conscienceless as all that. Come now, you must give me a clue. Is she a relation? Part French, maybe? Lived abroad most of her life?"

"Possibly," was the unhelpful reply.

"What a closemouthed fellow you've got to be, Trev." There was a speculative gleam in Lord Arden's grey eyes. "But then I daresay you've got your eye on her yourself. Our tastes have always been remarkably like. Still, you must know she's not your type—not at all."

"And what, precisely, do you think is not my type?"

"Why, the price is too high, Trev. Marriage. Your aunt's standing guard, after all. No slip of the shoulder in this case, I'm afraid."

"Then why are you so eager to meet her?"

"Because I've taken it into my mind to marry. Actually, she's put it into my mind. You know that my Respected Parent has been growling at me the last decade at least to be married and get heirs. He's been throwing that insufferable Honoria Crofton-Ash at me this age. Fortunately, my mother believes that a young man must sow his wild oats."

"And so you have, Will. You've sown them with a vengeance."

"And here," Lord Arden rhapsodised, quite deaf to his companion, "is the most beautiful woman I've ever seen. Though she was across the street, stepping out of the dressmaker's, your aunt hurried her into the carriage as though all the demons of Hell were after them."

"She only saw you coming, Will—"

"I could tell she was no schoolroom miss, and I had nearly resigned myself to one day being leg-shackled to some green girl fresh out of the nursery—and they're all so much alike, one Season after another, that you'd think Almack's baked them from a single mold. Well, I can only thank my lucky stars I obliged my sister by taking her into town. It's the greatest piece of good luck."

The man was insufferable. He'd only glimpsed Miss Ashmore from across the street and promptly decided to take possession, as if she were a handsome stickpin he'd taken a fancy to at Rundell and Bridge's. What a coxcomb he was! Still, Basil only looked amused as he answered, "But you don't even know her yet, Will. I wouldn't count it good luck so soon. Suppose you find she's ill-natured?"

"She couldn't look like that and be ill-natured. It's completely impossible. And even if she is—why, I fancy I might find ways to put her in better temper."

The smirk on Will's conceited face might have goaded a lesser man to violence. Basil, however, only answered amiably, "Pray, my lord, do not enlighten me on your methods. You must consider my delicate sensibilities."

The smile broadened. "Delicate sensibilities, indeed. Oh, you are droll, Trev. Not changed a bit after all this time. And what have you been doing with yourself—what is it?—three years now? How time flies. But come. Though I can't take you to dinner—being so agreeably engaged elsewhere—I will have a glass or two with you, and you must tell me about these heroics of yours."

= 6 =

"ASHMORE? NOT SIR Charles's daughter?" Lord Arden asked in some surprise. Surely that walking piece of antiquity had not produced this Incomparable? "I've read your father's accounts with the greatest pleasure, Miss Ashmore."

The melting look he bent on her belied entirely his private opinion that it was the most boring stuff he'd ever had the misfortune to come across and that even sermons were better by half.

Not having expected quite so sudden or so intense an assault, Alexandra was momentarily disarmed. However, having never been easily melted—well, perhaps with one exception—she was able, quickly enough, to school her features into a polite smile before turning to be introduced to someone else.

It was a small group. In addition to the Deverells and Lord Arden, there was Major Wells, an old friend of Lady Bertram, and Sir Philip Pomfret, an old friend of Lord Deverell, with his wife, and Lord and Lady Tuttlehope. The latter was Henry Latham's eldest daughter.

While civilities were being exchanged, Alexandra tried to sort out what Aunt Clem had told her about the Deverells and their affairs. Lady Deverell had been secretly married to Harry Deverell some thirty years ago. Not long after, Harry had drowned, and the then-pregnant Maria had married Matt Latham, Henry's brother. Only Harry hadn't drowned, after all. Three years ago, he'd resurrected himself and come back to England to claim his title and reclaim his wife and daughter.

Half of Society, according to Aunt Clem, had decided that Lady Deverell had been a bigamist. The other half, apparently, had decided that Harry was two people: the one who'd drowned nearly thirty years ago, and the one who was now a fair-haired, handsome man in his early fifties and very much alive. At any rate, regardless which half of the ton had decided what, virtually all its members somehow found themselves accepting the languid Maria into their midst, her scandalous history dismissed as little more than another one of her eccentricities. As to Isabella, she was not only Harry's legitimate daughter, but Countess of Hartleigh as well, and even the highest sticklers could not exclude her.

It was Isabella that Basil had schemed to marry. Alexandra wondered what she was like. She must be handsome since both her parents were. But was she languid and absentminded like her mother or energetic and blunt like her father?

While Miss Ashmore was at her wondering, she was also curious about Lord Tuttlehope. Obviously devoted to his lovely blond wife, obviously not a rogue of even the mildest sort, and so inarticulate and shy he could hardly put a whole sentence together—how could he be, as Aunt Clem had asserted, Basil's very best friend?

Alexandra had little opportunity for further speculation because the friendly, talkative Lady Tuttlehope pounced immediately upon her, drawing her away from the others.

"Oh, how pleased I am to meet you at last!" the baroness burst out. "What an exciting time you must have had. I haven't been abroad once, you know, because Freddie wouldn't stir from England while that dreadful Napoleon was about. I can't monopolise you now, I know," (though she showed every intention of doing so) "because that would be monstrous rude. But you must come to tea one day soon."

Not that her ladyship could wait for that happy time. Even as Alexandra smiled acquiescence, her companion went on chattering like an eager schoolgirl. Wasn't it an odd coincidence how they'd run into Basil so far away? And wasn't it amazing that Basil was a hero now and practically reformed—or so her Papa claimed, while Freddie maintained that Basil was quite the same as ever, and her ladyship must debate this with herself at length. "But here," she said, pausing to catch her breath, "I'm running on frightfully. What did *you* think?"

Alexandra didn't know what to think and was somewhat taken aback by both the barrage and the sudden question. Not that this incommoded her interlocutor in the least. Lady Tuttlehope went on about Basil and about how Harry Deverell had wanted to shoot him, but his wife had convinced him otherwise, saying that it was a very long way back to India, and Harry had only just gotten home, and it was bad enough that he had drowned, but then to get himself hanged for murder was too tedious for words. While Alexandra struggled to keep in countenance—her companion's imitation of Lady Deverell was uncanny—the baroness was telling her how terribly disappointed Freddie was that Basil would not be joining them for dinner.

"Oh. Then he was invited?" Alexandra asked in the most offhand way.

"Well, actually, I don't know. Aunt Maria made such a mystery of everything. She's so clever, you know, though one would never think it. They're *all* clever—at least they were clever enough for Basil," she added, meaningfully. "But then, you know about that. I'm sure Aunt Clem has told you." Without giving Alexandra a chance to reply, she artlessly confessed that *she* was not clever at all. "And it's a good thing, too, or Freddie would never know what to say to me."

As Lady Tuttlehope went on to tell what Freddie *did* say, Alexandra, feeling rather giddy, let her attention stray occasionally to the others in the company. She noted that

Lord Arden had turned her way more than once, as though about to approach. Each time, Lady Deverell called his attention back to herself. Thus, when they sat down to dinner, Alexandra had still not formed any sort of opinion about him beyond the fact that he was a most attractive man whose attire could not be faulted.

Lord Arden, who found himself seated on the opposite side of the table from Miss Ashmore and down at the other end on Lady Deverell's right, was beginning to wish his languid hostess at the devil. Maria had placed him there deliberately to torment him. There was no way he could converse with Miss Ashmore at this great distance. He must perforce be content to hear Maria sigh at him now and then between sighs at Sir Philip, or to talk with Lady Pomfret, who only complained interminably of India when she wasn't complaining that there wasn't a cook in London who knew how to make a proper curry.

Well, if he couldn't talk, he could look, and there was feast enough for the eyes to make a man never eat again, although it must be admitted that Lord Arden did honour to his dinner, nonetheless. She was even more beautiful than he'd thought. What wicked chestnut curls, to tease themselves loose from their pins and make her look ever so slightly but oh so provocatively dishevelled. And those eyes. Quite emerald green—or darker even—with naughty gold specks that danced when she laughed. She was delicious. Though she hadn't said more than two words to him, he knew she was perfection, which obviously meant that she must be his wife.

This knowledge must console him as he lingered with the gentlemen over port—and they did linger, an unconscionably long time. When they'd finally done and moved on to the drawing room to join the ladies, Lord Tuttlehope drew him aside.

"I say, Will, odd thing, ain't it?"

"What is?" the marquess asked impatiently.

"Couldn't say a word back there—Harry, you know. But he ain't here, is he?"

"*Who* isn't here?" Really, Freddie could be the most exasperatingly slow fellow. A small crowd was forming around Miss Ashmore, and that made Lord Arden unhappy. Crowds were inimicable to private conversation, and besides, they blocked his view of her form, so tantalisingly outlined by the elegantly simple, sea-green gown she wore.

"Why, Trev." Lord Tuttlehope blinked in some surprise that Arden hadn't worked this out for himself. "Don't seem right when he went out of his way on her account. Could have come straight from Greece weeks ago. Least they could do is feed him, what?"

This was amazing eloquence from the inarticulate Freddie, and it seemed to have a point. "On whose account was he delayed, Freddie?"

"Her. Ashmore's girl."

Lord Arden patiently questioned Freddie more closely and learned that Basil knew Miss Ashmore and had travelled with her all the way from Albania. The sly devil had never even hinted at it through all the bottles they'd shared this afternoon. But then, why should the man make anything of it? Even Trev wouldn't dare toy with his aunt's goddaughter. He'd said nothing about the matter because there was nothing to say. They'd travelled together with her Papa and others, and that was all there was to it.

Having thus reassured himself, the marquess proceeded to ease Freddie's troubled feelings. "As to Trev not being asked, what did you expect? Harry must still bear a grudge for that business three years ago."

Lord Tuttlehope blinked at him in surprise.

"Come now, Freddie. All Society knows Lady Hartleigh is Harry's daughter. They've made no secret of it, and any number of us know that Basil was up to some nasty business concerning her that got him packed off to India."

With several more blinks, Lord Tuttlehope stoutly denied that this was so and then in the next moment contradicted himself by insisting that Harry didn't bear a grudge. At least, so his beloved Alicia had assured him.

"Then," said Lord Arden, glancing at Lady Deverell, who was smiling lazily at something Miss Ashmore was saying, "it must be Maria."

Leaving Lord Tuttlehope to puzzle out for himself what the languid Lady Deverell had to do with the matter, Will made his way to Miss Ashmore's side.

At the moment she was explaining to the assembled group some of the pitfalls into which the subtleties of Albanian had led her. He had leisure, therefore, to admire—in addition to everything else he'd noted before—her low, husky voice. It thrilled him.

"And so," she was saying, "to pronounce it one way was to call him a boy—and yet to accent it only a bit differently was to call him a fiend. And the poor thing, who'd been so kind to find the goat for us, could not understand why I scolded him."

"But as it was a little boy, surely he could think of a reason for being scolded," Lady Tuttlehope responded. "They are always up to some mischief or other."

Lord Deverell added, with some pride, "Why, my grandson's only a year old, and already a prodigy at crawling into devilment."

Interesting as such conversation must be for doting Grandpapas, it eventually came to an end, and the party broke off into smaller groups. In time only Lord Arden, Lady Tuttlehope, and Lady Deverell remained with Miss Ashmore, and soon, to the marquess's unutterable relief, even this number dwindled. Maria, bored finally with standing between himself and Miss Ashmore, making conversation impossible with her sighs and lazy drawls, took herself languidly away to chat with Lady Bertram. That left only Lady Tuttlehope to thwart him.

The baroness, who had a romantic heart, was torn between leaving these two stunning creatures alone and wanting to hear what they'd say to each other. The choice was made for her when she saw her husband trapped into conversation with Lady Pomfret. She exclaimed softly, "Oh dear. Freddie is blinking terribly. Please excuse me." And off she went to his rescue.

Smiling a little at Lady Tuttlehope's ingenuous ways, Alexandra looked up to find herself the object of a very appreciative gaze. He was, just as Aunt Clem had promised, devilishly handsome. His hair was dark as a raven's wing, gleaming blue-black in the candlelight. The strong, rugged angles of his face were softened by grey eyes that managed to look boyish and innocent—though his manner was too polished to be boyish, his gaze too warmly appraising to be innocent. His manner, in fact, reminded her very much of someone else.

"I daresay, Miss Ashmore, that all of Society will be interrogating you about the mysterious country you visited. In a week you'll be sick to death of it and must swoon at the mere mention of the place."

The killing look he bent upon her would have invited a weaker-minded female to swoon in any case, but Alexandra was made of sterner stuff. "Surely there's no danger of that, my lord. My simple reports cannot compete with Lord Byron's romantic tales, and Society, I am sure, has got those by heart."

"You credit Society with longer memory than it possesses—at least on any matter not fraught with scandal. And even if people had got the stories by heart, they would prefer—at least the gentlemen would, I know—to hear of the place from the lips of a beautiful lady."

"Would they? How odd." She looked up at him in a puzzled way. "Oh," she said in soft surprise, as though she'd only then caught his meaning. "You meant that as a compliment."

"It's the simple truth, Miss Ashmore. Byron himself would second me. That cannot surprise you, surely. I daresay that even Basil required you to spin tales for him by the hour—and he likes nothing better than to hear *himself* talk."

She looked puzzled again, and he explained hastily, "I thought you and your father travelled with Mr. Trevelyan. Perhaps I misunderstood?"

"Oh. Why, yes, he did accompany us on our return." Lord Arden looked rather sly, she thought, and she wondered what Basil may have said about her. Surely he wouldn't have boasted of stolen kisses. And was the marquess another such? Did he mean to work his arts upon her, too? She looked away from him, seeking a polite means of escape from this suddenly depressing exchange. But the others were engrossed in their own conversations, and Lord Arden was talking again.

"Yes, well, I couldn't be sure. Basil never said a word. It was only Freddie who mentioned it just a moment ago. As a matter of fact, Miss Ashmore, no one would say a word. They've all contrived to make a mystery of you, as though you'd dropped from out of the heavens into London."

The slyly inquisitive look disappeared, and with it her discomfort. They could not all be Basil Trevelyans. Besides, Aunt Clem would never have specially arranged for her to meet a scoundrel. Smiling at her unwonted timidity and mistrust—although his lordship took the smile as intended for himself—she answered, "Well, I'm not at all mysterious. I was abroad for six years with my father— and not in the most civilised places. Most likely I was such a ragamuffin upon my return that no one wanted to admit my existence until I could be made to look respectable again."

Lord Arden opened his mouth to contradict, eagerly, this slight upon her charms but was prevented by the reappearance of Lady Deverell, who had drifted back to them.

"How tiresome of me," she announced, with inexpressible ennui. "I had quite forgotten what I meant to ask you before, Will. It was that recipe for curry Lady Pomfret explained at such length that distracted me, I'm sure. It was so absorbing, was it not?"

Lord Arden agreed soberly that it was most absorbing.

"And if I'd realised it troubled her so, I would have asked Auguste to make it—although it is likely Harry would have left the house. He declares he cannot abide to see another curried anything again for as long as he lives. My husband," she explained to Miss Ashmore, "spent many years in India. But what was I about?" She stared thoughtfully at her diamond bracelet and must have found the answer there, for in a moment she told them, very wearily indeed, "Oh, yes. Isabella. How tiresome she is, Will."

"Not a bit of it. She's perfectly delightful."

"Yes, that is what I meant. She is so determinedly delightful that it quite wears me out to contemplate it. But she insists that I come to Hartleigh Hall at last, and so I must go, I suppose. And she declares she must have you, too, Will, and Jess—for if you don't bring your sister, you can't come at all, poor dear. The children will never forgive you, such hard-hearted creatures they are."

Lord Arden was delighted to accept and promised less delightedly to bring his sister.

"It will not be a very large party—such a pity your parents are in Scotland, though I daresay it's more comfortable for them. At any rate, Lady Bertram comes, of course, with Miss Ashmore." She did not appear to notice Miss Ashmore's little start. "And Freddie and Alicia. Oh, yes. Lady Bertram promises to write your Papa, Miss Ashmore—and that young man who assists him. She said he was very pleasant."

Lord Arden's eyes might have been perceived to narrow ever so slightly.

"Though where to write them is the great question. If he has gone on to visit the Burnhams in Yorkshire, he will hardly wish to travel so far in this heat for a quiet house party among so many strangers. Yet I was positive Henry Latham meant to have him to Westford. At any rate, that is all, I suppose, though one cannot be certain with curry uppermost in one's thoughts."

The prospect of meeting her father at Hartleigh Hall with Randolph in tow was not pleasant to contemplate. Very sensibly, then, Alexandra put it out of her mind. It was not sensible, however, to feel so very disappointed that a certain name was conspicuously absent from the guest list. She forced a smile as she told her two companions she was looking forward to making so many new acquaintances.

"Well, I only hope we do not wear you out, Miss Ashmore. You have just got to London"—a perfectly heart-breaking sigh—"and now you must be dragged off again. You have only had a very little respite from Basil and now must be thrust into his company once more." Lady Dever-ell shook her head sadly over this, as one who could not account for the naughty behaviour of Providence.

"Then Basil is coming as well?" Lord Arden asked with a covert glance toward Miss Ashmore.

"Why yes. Didn't I say so? Well, perhaps I didn't. That curry plagues me so." And with another tragic sigh, the viscountess floated away.

=7=

"So," BASIL WAS saying, as he played with the note he'd received that morning—nearly a week after the dinner to which he'd not been invited. "It isn't enough they bid me come and be roasted by all my relations at once, but they must have Will, too, and Jess. Well, we know what that's all about, don't we?"

Freddie didn't know, but he nodded sagely nonetheless.

"And if they mean to push her off on the first peer who comes along, it's not my trouble is it?"

Freddie shook his head.

"Arden's welcome to her. But I am not about to keep Jess amused while he woos Miss Ashmore. I'm not Hartleigh's court jester, after all."

Freddie was halfway into a nod but stopped suddenly and blinked instead. "Don't mean you're not coming?"

"I am not."

"But they ain't seen you in three years, and we're going."

"I'll be very sorry to lose your company, Freddie, but my family must learn that I am no longer to be ordered about, here and there, at their whim. Why, they make up some claptrap about a young woman in dire straits and dispatch me off to rescue her. Dire straits. I'll tell you who's in dire straits—anyone who comes within a mile of her tongue, that's who."

"Seemed amiable enough to me. Alicia likes her."

"Freddie, your beautiful wife is so good-natured that she can discover no less in all those she meets."

Such praise could not fail to gratify one who saw his wife as the paragon of every sort of perfection and virtue. Even so, Freddie could not willingly forego his friend's company. He made a stammering attempt to change Basil's mind.

"No, Freddie, I can't do it. I'll see you in another month or so, no doubt, when you come back to town. I will not play the fool again, even to accommodate *you*. Besides, I have business to attend to."

"Business? This time of year?"

"Oh, yes. I must see about a house, of course, for I don't intend to live in a hotel forever. But more important, I've just met a perfectly charming barque of frailty, and if I go away now, there are half a dozen others ready to take my place in her mercenary affections. Such business cannot wait. Jess must contrive to entertain herself, and you must find consolation in the company of your beautiful wife."

Lord Tuttlehope returned home bluedevilled. He was the happiest of husbands, but he'd missed his clever friend dreadfully. Now to learn that he must endure that friend's absence until the Little Season at least . . . There was no understanding Basil lately. They'd only seen him twice in the two weeks since he'd returned. It was most disappointing, and so he told his wife.

"Oh, Freddie," she said, "whatever are you thinking? Of course Basil is coming."

"Not at all. Said he wasn't."

"Oh, he never means half what he says. You know that, dear. Maria says he'll be there, and so he will."

Lady Deverell, of course, knew everything. Quite like Lady Bertram in that respect. A couple of oracles they were. Nonetheless, Freddie stoutly maintained that Basil would not appear. "*She'll* be there, you know, and he can't abide her."

"Whom do you mean, darling?"

"*Her.* Ashmore girl."

"Basil can't abide her?" Lady Tuttlehope's eyes opened

wide with astonishment. "But she's so beautiful—and so clever and amiable."

"Hates her," her husband insisted. "Said so. Won't be made a fool of."

"So that's why he hasn't gone to see his aunt. Yet, what kind of excuse is it, when he's been away three whole years? Then I hope he shan't come after all, the mean thing. For he's sure to be unpleasant to Miss Ashmore, and then I shall have to hate him. I think she's lovely, and I hope she marries Will. Did you see the way he looked at her the other night? It made my heart flutter."

Lord Tuttlehope was a generous-minded man, but he did not like his wife's heart to flutter on anybody's account but his own. He blinked unhappily, and the tactful Alicia moved quickly to reassure him.

"Oh dear," she said, after a few very pleasant minutes had passed.

"What? What is it?"

"You came home looking so troubled, dear, that I forgot all about Marianne's letter."

"All well, I hope," her husband responded, though he really couldn't care less at the moment. He wanted more coddling.

"Quite well. Though she does say Mama has been very tiresome about her coming to us for a Season. Poor girl— she'd so much rather stay at home with her books."

"Quiet, sensible girl." Lord Tuttlehope dimly remembered Marianne as the least terrifying of Alicia's three younger sisters.

"Yes. And she writes to say that Papa has brought guests with him. You'll never guess."

"Can't think who."

"Miss Ashmore's Papa. And a young man—a Mr. Burnham. Very agreeable, Marianne says. He knows heaps about old things—history, you know, dear—and must talk the livelong day about it, for she crossed an entire page telling me about the something wars. It begins with a 'p,' I think—something like 'Penelope'—but it's much too hard a word to remember."

Her husband couldn't think what it was either and didn't especially want to know. He had much rather be assured again about Lord Arden and so found a way to stammer back to that subject and be comforted accordingly.

The post must have been doing a brisk business that day, for Alexandra also had a letter from Westford. It was not from Marianne Latham—Alexandra didn't know that young lady—but from Sir Charles. And, as was the case with most of the baronet's communications, it was annoying.

The long and the short of it was that he'd found out that Mr. Trevelyan was a perfectly dreadful young man. Sir Charles had found it out from Mrs. Latham, who, in the course of apprising him at unnecessary length of her dear daughter Alicia's highly satisfactory marriage to a baron, had also some choice words to bestow on the subject of the baron's good friend, Mr. Trevelyan.

"And it's no good," wrote Sir Charles in his crabbed script, "that Mr. Latham makes excuses for him. Nor can I think what excuse to make for *you*, Alexandra. Trevelyan is, and has been for all his adult life, one of London's most notorious libertines. I must believe you either the greatest fool or the most deceitful daughter there ever was. How, I ask, could the man be secretly engaged to you when three years ago he was so busy trying to get himself engaged to Mr. Latham's niece—or former niece—I cannot make out what the relations are in that family. Everywhere I turn, I hear nothing but scandal. If I were not kept here on important business, as Mr. Latham expresses interest in investing in my Albanian work, I would come and take you away immediately. Still, while I am here some matters can be put in train, and in a few more days I expect that Randolph and I can come to London for you."

There was more, a great deal more, and all of it unpleasant. Alexandra was scowling at the letter when Lady Bertram entered the room. "Good heavens, child, what dreadful news is it?"

The younger woman made no answer, but simply handed over the document so she might see for herself. Lady Bertram read it, glared, then crumpled the letter in a ball and tossed it into the cold fireplace. "Don't trouble yourself, my dear," she said. "No one is going to cart you off anywhere like so many bushels of corn. You're in England now, Alexandra, and among friends."

"But Papa—"

"—is only in bad humour because he hasn't any bits of ancient rubble to be poking at. This is nothing to distress yourself about. Go now. Will arrives shortly to take you for a drive, and you haven't even begun to dress. I will send Emmy up to you directly."

Smiling, Alexandra pointed out that it did not require two full hours to make herself ready.

"Then find something to do, there's a dear girl. I must write some letters.'

Ordinarily, Lord Arden would not have taken his Intended to Hyde Park—certainly not at five o'clock—since this would announce her existence to every bachelor still in town. Fortunately, the party was scheduled to leave for Hartleigh Hall the following day. He trusted, therefore, that when she next appeared in the park, it would be as his wife. What a glorious marchioness she'd make! And when the Respected Parent finally stuck his spoon in the wall, she'd make an even more stupendous duchess.

Accordingly, Lord Arden set himself to being even more agreeable than usual, though it scarcely seemed possible, and suppressed his boredom when she firmly turned the conversation from gossip to politics. Nor did he patronise her (at least not very much) when she went on to talk so earnestly of literature, though he didn't listen either. He was too busy imagining what it would be like to have a beautiful bluestocking as his hostess. Fondly, he pictured her astonishing his aristocratic colleagues with her harangues. He even envisioned her teaching an assortment of handsome children—some green-eyed, some grey-eyed—to lisp Greek and Latin.

Yes, a beautiful wife who was slightly eccentric was even better than a beautiful wife who was much like everyone else. Thus, though he barely heard five words out of every twenty, he fancied he was quite in love with her mind as well as everything else about her.

In this state so closely approaching the platonic ideal, he felt generous towards his fellows. His heart went out to the elegant gentlemen who stopped to stare as they drove past. He especially pitied his cronies who charged at them every few minutes, greeting him so warmly and begging to be made known to his attractive companion. It was only when Trevelyan appeared that this spirit of generosity ebbed away.

Trev was polite, certainly. But Lord Arden did not care for the way those devious cat eyes raked over Miss Ashmore, especially since that raking made the lady turn colour and lose her composure—and more especially since nothing his lordship had said or done had aroused so strong a reaction. It was, moreover, some time before she fully recovered. After Basil left, she seemed to have some trouble putting her sentences together—she who'd been so eloquent on the subject of Mr. Wordsworth only moments before.

His lordship was determined to help her along. "And so what do you think will become of Byron's poetry now that he's married?" he asked. "Do you think that wedded bliss will dull his sharp tongue?"

She appeared to shake herself out of a trance to answer him. "I haven't yet had an opportunity to read very much of his work. But from what I've heard recently, there's little bliss in that marriage."

"I fear you're right. But then, many of us maintain that

he was bound to make a poor husband. Some are improved, even reformed, by marriage. Others, like Byron, are only made worse by it."

It occurred to her that perhaps it was not really Lord Byron he was speaking of, but someone else. Yet her features remained blank as she asked him to explain.

"Because it makes them feel 'cabin'd, cribb'd, confin'd.' And so they must run away to lose themselves in some desperate pursuit of pleasure."

"You speak so knowingly, my lord. Do you, too, view marriage as a prison?"

"Ah, you mean to trick me, Miss Ashmore. For if I say I do not, you'll throw my long bachelorhood in my face. And if I say I do—why, then, what will you conclude about my intentions towards yourself?"

Such a query was meant to be answered in one way only: with a coy claim of ignorance. His lordship then enlightening her in proper form—perhaps on bended knee, though it would be deuced awkward in the phaeton—the matter would be settled. Miss Ashmore might then turn her thoughts to her trousseau, and he—why, to any of those myriad subjects far too taxing for the minds of young ladies.

But Lord Arden received no claim of ignorance, coy or otherwise. Miss Ashmore stared at him for a moment as though he had asked whether he might stand on his head. Then, in the voice of a schoolmistress, she answered, "I would not presume to judge your lordship's behaviour or intentions, and most especially not on such *short acquaintance*. It was only your opinion I sought."

The emphasis she placed on the words told him plainly that he'd leapt ahead of himself and had better leap right back. He had not expected this setdown, but then he reminded himself that she was a tad eccentric after all, and that was one of her charms. And so, the obedient student gave it as his opinion that marriage improved partners who were well suited and worsened those who were not. In

Byron's case, he went on, there was a moody, restless nature to begin with and too-early fame and adulation to compound the problem. In fact, he pointed out, if all those who shouldn't think of marrying didn't, it would be easier for better-suited persons to find each other.

"You think then," she asked, "that these ineligible individuals should be driven from Society? Or perhaps should be made to wear a badge of some sort to warn the unwary away?"

He chuckled. "That would be an extreme solution—and yet, perhaps it might conduce to greater happiness all around."

He dropped a deeply meaningful glance upon her, but she only appeared thoughtful as she added, "And thereby contribute to the greater prosperity of the British nation. What a novel idea, my lord. It does you credit, I am sure."

The prosperity of the nation was the very last thing on his mind, but he did not object to taking credit where it was not due. It was his aim, was it not, to win her admiration or respect or affection or whatever it might take to install her as quickly as possible as his marchioness. Therefore, despite the unexpected check to his impatient aspirations, his lordship passed the remainder of his time with her in remarkably good humour.

Mr. Trevelyan, lounging at his club, was not in good humour. He had a glass of very old brandy in his hand, and he glowered at it. His severe, black and white evening attire was perfect in every deceptively simple detail, and he scowled precisely as though these were the same filthy rags he'd worn in Gjirokastra. He had an appointment for dinner with a lovely blond barque of frailty, and he looked forward to it with the same cold composure with which he would, in earlier days, have awaited an interview with one of his creditors. Mr. Trevelyan, in short, was very cross.

Miss Ashmore had not, as any right-minded woman would—considering the trouble he'd taken on her account—greeted him with anything like enthusiasm. She'd turned rather pink, then rather white, and then had stared at him for an instant as though he were some great hulking monster. Then she'd turned to that snake beside her and let him do the talking for her, as though she belonged to him already. Clearly, Will seemed to think so. He had that proprietary air and that obnoxious, self-satisfied smirk on his arrogant face, and had even found it necessary—the great coxcomb—to lean close to speak to her as though the girl were quite deaf.

It was disgusting . . . and pathetic. The ridiculous chit had gone and put herself into the hands of one of the most—if not *the* most—untrustworthy, fickle, careless, self-ish, and *depraved* men in England. Oh, yes, Will meant to marry her, but marriage meant nothing to him. He'd get his precious heirs on her and then be off about his usual lecheries.

Whatever was Aunt Clem thinking, to countenance the man? Surely she knew what he was. Aunt Clem sees all, knows all. Had she simply balanced off the brute's character against his material assets? It would, after all, be a great thing to marry off her goddaughter to a future duke. Single, good-looking dukes were rare, and single, good-looking dukes with vast fortunes were scarcer than hen's teeth. No, she could hardly do better than Will.

Still, Aunt Clem might have found an eligible *parti* with a better character. But then, what was it to him? Certainly he wasn't about to look out for a better husband for Miss Ashmore, and he most definitely was not about to go haring off to Hartleigh Hall just to make certain she didn't get into any trouble. Let her get herself out of trouble this time, the ungrateful wench.

He reached into his breast pocket and pulled out the letter he'd already read some five or six dozen times, and crumpled it angrily in his hand. Then, in the next moment, he just as angrily smoothed it out again, folded it, and tucked it back into his pocket. She might at least have smiled.

=8=

ALEXANDRA SIGHED AS she approached the breakfast room. She'd thought that the fresh country air would cure her sleeplessness, but the past five nights at Hartleigh Hall had been exactly like those preceding. When finally she did fall asleep, she had very troubling dreams. The gallant knights who rescued her from dragons that looked like the Burnham sisters kept turning out to have deceitful, amber eyes instead of adoring, grey ones.

Because she hadn't slept properly since she'd come to England, she was prey to headaches, one of which was now shooting sharp blasts of pain behind her dark eyebrows. The great racket coming from the breakfast room promised only to exacerbate it. Perhaps she'd better turn back and have breakfast sent up to her room.

Unfortunately, Burgess, Lord Hartleigh's terrifying butler, had already seen her approach. She was astonished to note faint creases, ominously hinting at a smile, at the corners of his mouth. And then—good heavens—he was actually opening the door for her himself.

She winced slightly at the Babel of voices, but in an instant her eyes flew wide open. There at the breakfast table, smiling with complete self-assurance at some sarcasm Lord Hartleigh directed at him, was the inconsiderate creature who haunted her dreams. He'd turned towards the door as it opened, and when his gaze locked with hers it carried all the impact of a physical blow. The other faces were dissolving into haze, the voices into a buzzing in the background, and all she saw was the slow smile that lit his wicked face. Then he spoke, and the familiar, insinuating sound shook her out of her daze.

"Thank heaven you've come, Miss Ashmore—and in the very nick of time. They're all lined up against me, and I want an ally badly."

"What's this?" Lord Deverell exclaimed. "Was India so taxing then? Are you so enfeebled that you require a woman's help to speak?"

"Ah, but I always require the ladies' assistance—"

"Oh, he hasn't changed a bit," someone murmured, but Alexandra barely noticed. He was still looking at her and talking.

"Luckily, Miss Ashmore has most kindly made it her business to look out for me."

She hadn't time to blush, being too busy thinking—and that wasn't the most agreeable exercise with her head throbbing so. How dare he say such things in front of these others? Lord Arden had leapt to help her to her chair, and she used the moment that gave her to collect her wits. His lordship placed her conveniently next to himself and inconveniently opposite Mr. Trevelyan. There was nothing for it then but to meet those glittering, feline eyes calmly. "I'm sorry, sir," she finally answered, "but I don't recollect undertaking any such formidable task. At any rate," she went on more briskly, "you can't expect one to do business of any sort before breakfast."

"Certainly not," Lord Deverell agreed. "Will, don't stand there gawking. Fill Miss Ashmore's plate for her."

It could not have been agreeable for Lord Arden to be ordered about by a mere viscount, as though he were an awkward schoolboy. On the other hand, it may have been the unwelcome addition to the company that made his lordship scowl so horribly as he stood at the sideboard selecting the choicest tidbits for his future wife and listening to the conversation.

"Well then, Miss Ashmore," Basil was saying. "I'll leave

you to fortify yourself, though it means fending off this great company singlehanded."

Lady Hartleigh laughed. "Don't even think of fending us off, Basil. Not when you've been so mean to tease and say you wouldn't come. But what is this great piece of nonsense you tell of Miss Ashmore?"

"It isn't a bit of nonsense," came the injured reply. "The whole while we travelled, Miss Ashmore was busy saving me from myself—and it was an uphill task, I assure you."

"And a thankless one, I make no doubt," his aunt put in.

The plate was set down before Miss Ashmore with an angry *thunk*.

"I wonder, Basil," said Lady Jessica, "how you came to need saving from yourself."

There was a deafening chorus of answers to this, most to the effect that Basil had needed to be saved from himself since the day he was born, that no one could do it, and that it must be given up as a bad job.

Alexandra was relieved that she wasn't left to deal with him all by herself, though their good humour surprised her. Hadn't he wronged at least four of these people? Still, his machinations had simply hurried Lady Hartleigh into her husband's arms and Lady Deverell back into those of her beloved Harry. It was rather, as Aunt Clem had claimed, a great joke. Basil's plots had succeeded only in getting him packed off to India.

"As to you, Miss Ashmore," Lady Jessica went on with studied innocence, "whatever possessed you to take on this monumental task?"

Alexandra very nearly choked on the fragment of toast she'd put in her mouth, but she managed to swallow it and answer calmly enough. "I daresay it must seem odd. But then, Albania has few amusements for an Englishwoman, and there's little enough to do on a long sea voyage. Papa and Mr. Burnham had their theories and writing to occupy them. I, on the other hand, had nothing. I suppose," she added, with a little shrug, "since Mr. Trevelyan is the very soul of honesty and he says I took on the job, then I must have—no doubt because I was so unspeakably bored."

Most of the company smiled appreciatively at this. At the other end of the table, Lady Deverell chuckled softly.

"Poor Basil," said Lord Hartleigh pityingly. "Only a diversion."

Lord Arden found the exchange a deal less amusing than the others and endeavoured to return Miss Ashmore's attention to himself. "Yet who would not delight to be Miss Ashmore's diversion?" he asked, sweetly.

"My lord," she chided, "you play into Mr. Trevelyan's hands."

"I?"

"Yes. You help him draw the fire to me and away from himself."

His disloyal sister joined in. "She's right, Will. We were all scolding him. Then you must say pretty things to Miss Ashmore and make everyone stare at her."

"When of course, dear sister, you'd rather they looked at you."

"Naturally—in good time. Now, however, it's Basil must bear our stern scrutiny. He's been most unkind to his family." The look she directed at Basil would have been severe indeed, except that her eyes—amazingly like her brother's—twinkled with mischief. "Let's hear his excuse."

"Yes, you young jackanapes," Lady Bertram growled. "What can you have to say for yourself? Nearly a fortnight in London and not once do you call on your aunt."

"Dearest Aunt, if I called on you I might have stumbled upon Miss Ashmore as well, and she told me to keep away."

"Abominable creature!" Lady Hartleigh cried. "You blame Miss Ashmore for everything."

"But isn't that so, Miss Ashmore? Didn't you tell me to keep away until further notice? For my own good?"

Alexandra's green eyes flashed dangerously. He wanted to embarrass her, the beast. Spreading a dab of butter on her toast, she answered coolly, "How, I wonder, could I make it my business to look out for you on the one hand while I drove you off on the other? How could I look out for you when you were not about?"

"Why, I don't know. I really can't understand it. Usually, you're so logical. I'm sure I've mentioned that before—how logical you are."

Alexandra was seriously considering throwing the coffee urn, an ornate, silver monstrosity, at him—how dare he remind her of that conversation in Prevesa?—when Lady Deverell's bored voice was heard. "I cannot make it out at all, and it makes my head ache, Harry. After all, if—as he says—Miss Ashmore told him to keep away, then why is the tiresome boy here?"

Lord Deverell only shrugged and smiled while Lord Hartleigh turned to his cousin and gravely asked what answer he had for that?

"Why, cousin, it must be obvious." Basil stared at him in mock astonishment that he couldn't answer this simple riddle.

Alexandra's mind raced as she imagined a hundred different answers he might make—all of them disconcerting—and her own hundred possible setdowns.

"None of you can guess?" He turned that wondering, childlike look on all of them in turn. "But it's so simple." His gaze rested then on Alexandra, and something in his eyes made her heart skid to a stop. "Amnesia," he said softly.

In the din that greeted this she breathed a small sigh of relief. Though Lord Arden was looking at her rather strangely, he held his tongue, and she was able to finish her breakfast in relative peace.

There was peace after breakfast as well, for she went riding with Lady Jessica, Lord Arden, and the Deverells. The older couple rode well behind, but with Jess there to contradict and mock him, Lord Arden was forced to keep the conversation general. Alexandra could let her mind wander freely, the intense exchange between brother and sister precluding any real participation.

She'd thought Lord Arden the answer to her prayers. He was handsome and amiable, and he appeared to be intelligent, even if he did look at her in that unnervingly proprietary way. After all, he'd been brought up to believe the universe was basically his for the taking.

The Burnhams wanted a daughter-in-law who could help them claw their way into the ton, but if Papa paid his debt in gold they'd have to be content with that. Lord Arden could easily afford to settle matters with them, and even Papa couldn't object to a future duke as son-in-law. Yes, Lady Bertram had selected well of all the eligible gentlemen she might have invited to take notice of her goddaughter. Even his sister was delightful. Why then, had he suddenly become so irritating?

"How quiet you are, Miss Ashmore," said Lady Jessica. "But how can you help it? Neither of us lets you get a word in edgeways."

"Speak for yourself, Jess. It's you who monopolise the conversation."

"Because otherwise you tease her—and that's too unfair when she was teased unceasingly at breakfast."

"As, to your mortification, you were *not*."

"I'm sure," Alexandra put in, "it'll be Lady Jessica's turn to be teased next. And as her performance is bound to be superior, I expect to learn a great deal from it."

"Miss Ashmore, you want no tutoring. I daresay you've had enough experience of Basil to know that he's immune to setdowns. Even if he were not, who could bear to stop him from talking so beautifully wickedly?"

"My sister," Lord Arden said with annoyance, "is and has been, since her debut, entirely lost to propriety."

"Well, you would know, my dear brother, so much experience you have of impropriety."

"She has the mind of an infant," he went on doggedly, "and exaggerates silly bits of gossip into great scandals—"

"On the contrary, I must reduce them to mere scandal in order to contemplate them—"

His lordship was growing exasperated. It had been vexing enough to find Trevelyan at the breakfast table this morning and to be forced to sit quietly as the man flirted outrageously with the future Marchioness of Arden. Now, here was one's own sister, holding up one's rather murky private life for Miss Ashmore's examination.

Still, Miss Ashmore did not seem horribly shocked. It occurred to him that he actually knew very little of his Intended—except that she was eminently desirable. She'd kept him at arm's length, and he'd been patient knowing that these genteel virgins did like to be courted forever. Yet, Trevelyan's insinuations had not once elicited any of those cool, reproving looks his own more gentle hints customarily evoked. For all her cool composure, she'd seemed different somehow, as though she'd been lighted up from within, the moment she'd clapped eyes on the wretch.

As to the expression on Trevelyan's face—that predatory look so appropriate to those feline eyes—one knew that look all too well. It promised, at the very least, complications. Lord Arden wanted no complications. This courtship business was time-consuming enough as it was. And where the devil was her blasted father?

"Well, Maria," said Lord Deverell, "he's exactly as you described. I've never met a more ingratiating villain, though I can't understand what makes me like him in spite of my better judgement."

"Really, my dear? Then why, I wonder, did you look at him so thunderously?"

Her husband smiled. "It was too much temptation. When I saw him try to draw her aside after breakfast, I couldn't resist stepping in his way. After all, I was unable to do so three years ago."

"Well, you glowered at him sufficiently to make up for that oversight. How naughty of you, Harry."

Lord Deverell laughed. "He didn't seem in the least intimidated. What, I ask, is this scheming devil about?"

"The poor boy is starved for attention. And no wonder, after three years among foreigners in climates you yourself have pronounced fit only for vermin."

"Attention is it? I rather think it's something else he's starved for. Or someone else. He looked exactly as though—"

"Please, my love. No vivid analogies. It is too early in the day to tax my mind so."

"You needn't waste your die-away airs on me, my lady. I know better. And I wish *you* did as well, for I can see there's bound to be trouble."

Maria sighed. "There always is, I'm afraid."

"You and Clementina between you have put the cat among the pigeons."

"Yes, love. And who are the poor pigeons, I wonder?"

He'd come, Basil told himself, only because London was so stupefyingly dull at the moment. The blond barque of frailty he'd managed to entice away from her protector had proved to be, upon closer examination, both vulgar and witless, and he'd been obliged to entice her back into protection again. Anyhow, there was bound to be better sport watching Arden, who'd never had to woo anyone in his whole life, woo Miss Ashmore. It had been great fun to annoy him at breakfast and to see the difficulty with which he controlled his rage when he saw how easily Miss Ashmore's attention could be diverted.

And Miss Ashmore? For all her cool self-possession, there was murder in her eyes. Basil had hoped she'd rip up at him afterwards, but Harry Deverell had come in the way. Then Isabella was ordering him up to the nursery to admire little Gerald, and after that Basil had to visit the schoolroom because, her ladyship insisted, Lucy would never settle down to her studies otherwise.

Well, he went, and the Hartleighs' adopted daughter was nearly as excited about seeing him as she was about the lovely dark-haired doll he'd brought her. Unfortunately, he must then debate with the child whether it most closely resembled Lady Jessica or Miss Ashmore. Lucy pointed out that Miss Ashmore was even prettier than Lady Jess and that her stories were every bit as wonderful as Mama's. It was, therefore, Lucy's considered opinion that this paragon should marry Lord Arden since she was as beautiful as a princess and he was very nearly a prince.

"A duke, you know," she explained patiently. "is *almost* a prince, and Miss Ames says he will be a duke one day."

Miss Ames stepped in at this point to remind Lucy that she was gossiping, and gossip was better left to one's elders. Leaving the governess to explain why this was so, Basil exited the school room feeling inexplicably put-upon.

Nor did his mood lighten when he responded to a summons from Aunt Clem. No doubt his aunt meant her lecture to be uplifting, but as he stood there, enduring what appeared to be an interminable scold on virtually every subject under the sun, he only felt more ill-used.

What she lectured about, Basil hardly knew. He'd never attended before and saw no reason to start now. There was something about the Burnham business and some cryptic comments concerning one of those Latham chits and any number of blistering references to her nephew's incompetence. All that did matter was that she made it impossible for said nephew to catch up with Will and his riding companions. When he'd finally escaped his aunt, Basil found that everyone else, including the traitorous Freddie, had left the house as well.

He'd been completely abandoned. The only ones to show any interest in his reappearance were the children; and the baby had fallen asleep three minutes after meeting his cousin, while ten-year-old Lucy found him a deal less fascinating than household gossip.

A fine welcome, he thought, as he stomped into the library and threw himself upon a great leather sofa. Gone three years, and they couldn't keep their minds on him past breakfast. And *she* needn't have dashed off in such a hurry to ride with Will. Basil had risked his life to rescue her, and she couldn't even take the time to scold him for teasing her.

It was odd that a gentleman who'd wished his aunt at the devil for wasting time scolding him should now be equally irate that another lady declined to do the same. But then, journeying some fifty miles in the dead of night can render the most even-tempered of men out of sorts and, consequently, illogical. At any rate, after spending another hour or so alone in the library, unable to concentrate on a book and quite disinclined to betake himself elsewhere, his temper began to fray. Small wonder he sought to take his frustrations out on the very next person he saw.

His sense of ill usage had reached a perfect fever pitch when, some hours later, the door to the library opened and Miss Ashmore wandered in, looking for the book she'd left there the evening before. She didn't see him at first because the sofa was nestled close to the bookshelves at the other side of the room, and her glance went immediately to a small table not far from the door. When he greeted her, therefore, she started, and one mischievous chestnut curl bounced playfully against her eyebrow. This enraged him past endurance. Abruptly he sat up and asked, in a voice dripping with sarcasm, whether she'd enjoyed her little jaunter with the marquess.

"Well, yes, I did, rather," she answered stiffly. "He and his sister were very amusing."

"Yes, you couldn't ask for a better sister-in-law than Jess."

"I don't recall having asked for one, Mr. Trevelyan," came the cold retort.

"Hadn't you? Well, my mistake. But I was certain that was what you'd asked Aunt Clem for. Sister-in-law. Brother-in-law. Any sort of in-law. So long as the last name wasn't Burnham."

She'd picked up her book and was half a mind to throw it at him but made herself reply evenly, "That was un-called-for, Mr. Trevelyan. As it is, however, entirely in keeping with your inconsiderate behaviour at breakfast, I must at least compliment you on your consistency."

"And I must compliment you on your alternative fiancé. Dear me, Will is a better catch than Randolph by a mile."

"Really?" she asked sweetly. "And even better than my *other* fiancé? Well, what a clever girl I am, to be sure." And she turned on her heel and left him.

He did not mean to let her have the last word, but the Fates conspired against him. After a light noonday meal, Edward insisted upon showing his cousin the divers im-provements made to the estate. This occupied them until teatime. During that meal, Miss Ashmore was engrossed in conversation with Will. Immediately thereafter, Basil was again commandeered by his cousin, along with Freddie and Lord Deverell, who demanded a complete account of his adventures abroad. Nor was there a suitable opportu-nity to get the last word that evening, for he could hardly quarrel with her across the whole length of the dinner table. Shortly after, Miss Ashmore took to her room, pleading a headache.

"I daresay Will gave it to her," Jess confided, as she plunked herself down upon the settee next to Basil. "He's such a bore playing the decorous suitor. Hasn't the first idea of what he's doing. No wonder he made her head ache."

"What a disloyal sister you are, Jess."

"Well, he's such a pest. He wants her attention every minute. Though it is diverting to see him so monstrous well behaved, especially when I know for a fact he's keeping not one, but two high flyers—twins, Basil, if you'll credit it—in London. And he's hardly dared kiss Miss Ashmore's hand."

The thought of those polluted lips upon Miss Ashmore's slender, virginal fingers was more than Basil could stomach. Because that particular image promptly conjured up any number of far more ghastly ones, he soon found that his dinner did not agree with him and made a rather early bedtime himself.

Lord Hartleigh sat propped against the pillows, watching his wife brush her fair, silky hair. She was even lovelier now than when he first knew her. Actually, the first time he saw her she hadn't been lovely at all, with her hair so primly pulled back and her dress so dowdy. But later, the night he'd first danced with her, she'd been lovely indeed. Another thought came to him and he frowned. "I don't like it, Isabella," he said. "Basil and Will under the same roof with that dazzling creature. Whatever was your mother thinking of?"

Lady Hartleigh moved from the dressing table to his side of the bed where she stood, gazing fondly at him. "It would appear," she answered with a wry smile, "that Mama has matchmaking in mind."

Her husband retorted that Lord Arden didn't appear to require any encouragement. "Those killing looks he drops on her make me want to howl."

"Still, I've seen him look that way at a hundred other women. Probably Mama thinks a little healthy competition will hurry him to the point."

"My cousin, I need not remind you, is hardly healthy competition. Did you see the way *he* looked at her?"

"Oh, it's just as he always does. She handled it with aplomb, I must say. Gave as good as she got—and among so many strangers, too. In her place I should have been covered in confusion."

"I think," Lord Hartleigh remarked, "I'd rather see you covered with kisses." He pulled her towards him, causing her to topple onto the bed, and immediately set to making action suit word.

"After all," he murmured sometime later, "it's not our problem, is it?"

"No, dear," came the faintly amused reply. "Not this time, thank heavens."

= 9 =

THOUGH HE DID not, precisely, sleep the sleep of the just, Basil must have achieved sufficient repose to improve his humour. Certainly, when the neighbourly Osbornes visited the following morning, he was most agreeable.

Not all the Osbornes graced Hartleigh Hall with their company. Jane was in bed with a cold, and James and his Papa were in London. But Hetty and the twins, Sarah and Susan, had come with their mother to improve their acquaintance with the single gentlemen currently residing at Hartleigh Hall.

Hetty had sulked the whole way over because, as she complained to her Mama, Lord Arden would look at no one but Miss Ashmore, and everyone knew Basil Trevelyan was the wickedest man alive. Within a very few minutes of her arrival, however, her spirits improved markedly. As he greeted her, Basil swept such an appraising glance over her as to make her cheeks turn bright red and then stared so besottedly into her brown eyes that she nearly reeled from the impact. Fortunately, being a steady sort of girl if not a particularly intelligent one, she recovered sufficiently to reward him with a coquettish smile.

"Never say that this Incomparable is little Hetty," Basil exclaimed to Mrs. Osborne, who'd watched these proceedings with mistrust. "You must have required an armed guard for her comeout to prevent her being killed in the crush of suitors." Mama's censorious frown wavered. "And you, ma'am, could not have escaped unscathed. For how on earth could the poor gentlemen know which was the daughter?"

Alexandra, who hadn't yet had the opportunity of observing Mr. Trevelyan try his skills upon anyone other than herself, was here provided an admirable opportunity to broaden her horizons. Oddly enough, she did not find the experience quite as pleasantly instructive as one would expect. She watched in grim fascination as, one by one, he reduced each of the three Osborne girls to giggling imbeciles, while simultaneously showering upon the Mama such sickeningly sweet droplets of flattery that even that stout, formidable matron became, in a matter of minutes, another trembling blossom athirst for the nourishing rain of his admiration.

The lesson was not at all improving to Miss Ashmore's temper, which had gotten a bad start at breakfast when she'd learned, along with everyone else, that her Papa had finally decided to accept Lady Hartleigh's gracious invitation and was arriving tomorrow afternoon. He was, moreover, bringing Randolph with him. If Alexandra had thought to forestall her father with hints about the future Duke of Thorne, it looked as though she'd better think again. Even as she watched, that undependable gentleman began competing with Basil for the twins' attention.

Lord Arden had not meant to do so. He had, in fact, been wracking his brains since yesterday, trying to contrive some means of getting Basil out of the way so that the courtship of Miss Ashmore might proceed apace. He'd been pleased to note that his Intended had scarcely said a word to Trev at breakfast. She'd apparently taken him in intense dislike, for she'd met the wretch's pleasantries with cool politeness and reserved her warm smiles for himself.

All the same, the marquess considered it neither natural nor agreeable to be completely ignored by a set of pretty young ladies under any circumstances, least of all in favour of Trevelyan. To correct this inequity, he insinuated himself into the conversation, and the twins soon rewarded him with blushes and giggles.

He did not, however, intend to take the duo driving in the afternoon. Unfortunately, Basil said something provoking—then the marquess retorted—then the twins looked so sweetly pleading . . . and, in the next minute the marquess found himself trapped in an engagement that would not win him any credit with his Beloved. He vowed inwardly to make speedy amends. But after admiring the dimple on Sarah's chin and noting its perfect mate upon Susan's, then bidding gallant goodbyes to them all, he turned around and found that Miss Ashmore had vanished.

When he asked his hostess where the young lady had gone, he learned that Miss Ashmore had promised Lucy an hour of her exclusive company.

"And you know, Will," Isabella reminded, "that Jess and Miss Ashmore must take her by turns, for she made them promise, and it's no good my telling them they spoil her dreadfully. Everyone spoils her, and poor Miss Ames is left with the thankless task of repairing the damage."

Lord Arden promptly took Lucy in violent dislike. Being a courteous gentleman, he did not share his feelings with his hostess or anyone else, though he did, shortly thereafter, find fault with his valet and berate that villain accordingly.

"You engineered that," said Lady Jessica accusingly, as she followed Basil out to the stables.

He replied very sweetly that he hadn't the faintest idea what she was talking about.

"Lud, will you listen to the man? He believes I'm a chawbacon, I think. You trapped him into driving those cabbageheads," she went on reproachfully. "I know you like to have your fun and show how clever you are, but this is not the time for it. What is Miss Ashmore to think?"

"That your brother's taste is faulty, perhaps?"

She shot him a shrewd look. "I think you want her for yourself."

"Of course I do. I want every lady for myself."

"And so you must make trouble for Will? Really, it's most unfair of you. This is the first time in his life he's ever shown the least bit of common sense."

"And a precious little bit it is when the first distraction that comes along is enough to knock it out of him. I don't know why you scold so, Jess. Why, you're the first to make sport of your brother. And now Miss Ashmore's seen him in his true colours, you're all in a fidge about it. Really, I'm surprised at you."

Lady Jessica Farrington was nobody's fool, and most especially not Basil's. Knowing him as well as she did her own brother, she was not about to be shrugged off so easily. It was true she didn't want to mislead Miss Ashmore. On the other hand, she didn't want Miss Ashmore alienated.

Lady Jess lived in lively terror that her brother would one day marry some beautiful, shallow, self-centered aristocrat like her own mother, totally incapable of improving Will in any way. He needed a great deal of improvement— and soon, if his character was not to be irretrievably ruined.

She'd believed that Miss Ashmore was capable of effecting the desired changes, if only Will didn't make her despise him. Which, of course, she was bound to do when she saw, not that he was a rake, for rakes were rather appealing, but that he was such a fickle creature that he couldn't even manage a pretence of keeping his mind on the woman he was courting.

In a few sentences she laid the matter out for Basil. "Don't you see?" she pleaded. "This may be his only chance to make something decent of himself."

"As he isn't my brother, I really don't care two sticks about it," was the unsympathetic reply.

"I should think," said the lady, "you'd enjoy seeing him taught a lesson—regardless your interest in his future."

"You know as well as I there's no teaching him anything."

They had reached the stables, but she drew him away, out of the grooms' hearing. "He's never been so vulnerable before, Basil. He does want to marry her, you know. Unfortunately, he has no experience in the business and doesn't know how to go on. That is to say, he just goes on as he always does—or will, unless Miss Ashmore sets him straight."

"Then what are you telling *me* for?"

"Because you must help her."

"No!" he snapped, with so much force that she was momentarily taken aback. "That is to say," he corrected hastily, "she wouldn't accept any help from me on any account. Nor do I think she'll take kindly to any advice from you on how to go on with your brother."

"If she were agreeable, would you help?" Jessica coaxed.

Idly tapping his riding crop against his leg, he considered this for a moment or two. Finally he replied, "Well, it would be a bit of fun to see that self-satisfied smirk wiped off Will's face."

She'd won her point, and pressed the advantage without waiting to hear more. "Good. Now, you're not going riding yet."

He protested that he was.

"No. You'll ride with *her*, this afternoon, while Will is out with the twins. We'll make sure he knows about it as soon as he returns. That should make him think twice about taking her for granted."

Deaf to Basil's ironical comments regarding her powers of persuasion, Lady Jess stepped away briefly to tell the grooms to have horses ready for Mr. Trevelyan and Miss Ashmore directly after nuncheon.

This done, she turned back to her victim. "Now you must go use all your wiles to persuade her to ride with you."

"I?" he asked indignantly. "I've only agreed to go along

with the scheme, if you can effect it. Didn't I just tell you she won't—"

"If she won't, then you're not the man you were. Even if she hates you, you must know some way to get round her, Basil. Lud, Will could do it without thinking half a minute." Lady Jess knew her man, after all. It wanted only the one hint—that Will's powers of persuasion were superior to his own—to effect complete capitulation. Basil agreed to do as he was told.

Though he knew Miss Ashmore's citadel was not to be so easily stormed, he resolutely waylaid her after she'd left the schoolroom and was descending the stairs. He proceeded to offer such a variety of abject apologies, with every possible expression of penitence, as well as some quite impossible ones, that he soon had her laughing in spite of herself. Having obtained a rather choked pardon for his inexcusable misconduct of the previous day, he then went on to the trickier business of coaxing her to ride with him.

He'd intended to goad her into it. If she refused, he'd say she was afraid of him and incapable of keeping one mischievous gentleman in order. But those green eyes, sparkling with amusement, drove his planned scenario right out of his head.

"Will you ride with me then?" he asked. Seeing her face stiffen, he went on hurriedly, "Jess is furious that her brother's abandoned you for a pair of idiots, and she's determined that you're to teach him a lesson and I'm to be the means. And though I don't especially care to do him any favours, what choice have I when this is the only way I might have your company all to myself?"

Alexandra looked away and addressed her remarks to the bannister. "I believe," she told that gleaming object, "this gentleman attempts to play on my wounded vanity and my unwounded vanity simultaneously."

"Of course I do. You know I'm the sort of man who stops at nothing."

"In that case, a sensible woman must forego your company, I think."

"Then don't be sensible, Miss Ashmore. I'd like nothing better than to ride with you. I've missed you horribly."

The words were no sooner out of his mouth than he urgently wished them back again. He heard them for what they were—Truth—and that wouldn't do at all.

Of course, she didn't believe him. Her face attested to that plain enough though she was still looking at the bannister. Yet, her reaction changed nothing. He *had* missed her horribly. Why else would he have given in so easily to Jess? Even now, as Alexandra hesitated, he was wondering what he would do if she refused. He was unable to invent a satisfactory answer.

"Well, I suppose you can't help it," she said finally, with a teasing smile that rather surprised him. "Though you momentarily forgot to mention it, the sun does rise and set on my fair countenance, and you can't sleep for thinking of me, and—what else?"

"And," he answered steadily, "if you don't come riding with me, I shall be the most miserable wretch that ever lived."

"Oh, yes. I wonder how that slipped my mind."

"Then you will ride with me?" he persisted.

What was she to do? He claimed to be sorry. He'd apologised in every way his fertile mind could invent. If she was willing to ride with others, wouldn't it look odd that she wouldn't ride with him? After all, he did claim it was Jess's idea, and one could always ask Jess about that. In short, after a little more hesitation, and a little more persuasion, Miss Ashmore convinced her mind to agree with her heart and consented.

Jessica pounced on him after nuncheon, as soon as he was alone. "Well? Have you done it?"

"Yes."

"Good. I knew you could. Now you must keep her out until teatime—later, if you can manage it. That'll have Will in a frenzy."

"Until teatime! What do you expect me to do? Tie her to a tree?"

"Get lost. Have your horse throw a shoe. Have it throw you. Surely you can think of something."

"I can think of a great many things," he answered, his face a perfect study in wickedness. "However, I understood it was your brother you wanted shackled—not me."

"Oh, stow it, Basil. If you keep her sufficiently amused, she won't notice the time passing."

Without waiting for any more evil hints of the amusements he contemplated, Lady Jessica took herself off to her sitting room and the latest publication from the Minerva Press awaiting her therein.

"Going riding, are you?" Lady Bertram enquired as she bestowed a look of approval upon her goddaughter's wine-coloured habit.

She'd been right to send the girl to Madame Vernisse. The modiste had settled upon simple, clinging lines in rich colours, ignoring the fussy furbelows currently in fashion, since they did not suit Miss Ashmore at all. Yes, Alexandra would do very well.

"Y-yes," came the nervous answer. "With Mr. Trevelyan."

"I see."

"Unless you think I shouldn't."

"Whyever not? Can't have Farrington thinking he's the only male in Creation, can we? You're quite right. Do him good. And Basil, too. The boy's so fidgety lately, he's bound to get into trouble out of sheer boredom. You'll be doing him a favour—not that he deserves it—but you know that. I don't need to tell you to box his ears if he misbehaves."

Alexandra, who'd been critically examining her gloves, looked up quickly. "Misbehaves?"

"I mean, child, if he behaves in any way you don't like. Which, as I said, I don't need to tell you."

Giving her goddaughter a kindly smile, the countess took herself away.

= 10 =

IF ALEXANDRA NEITHER noticed the time passing nor felt obliged to box the gentleman's ears, that was probably because her companion was behaving so well. He was entertaining, as usual, but in such a friendly, nonthreatening way that she felt much in charity with him as they ambled in leisurely fashion about the enormous estate.

Estate was hardly the word. With its great expanses of field and meadow, its gently rolling hills and rich valleys, its little ponds and waterways, the Hartleigh property was more like a small kingdom. The estate even had its own forest, an extensive stand of wood left much as Nature had made it, though the clear trails showed that the same care was given to this wilderness as to the rest of Lord Hartleigh's beautifully groomed domain.

She had certainly admired the estate during other rides but Basil took her along paths she hadn't travelled before and talked of childhood escapades, sharing his associations with this stretch of meadow and that golden field and this little duck pond. The stories vividly conjured the childhood of this puzzling man and helped her, at least to some extent, to understand him better.

He had, naturally, been into mischief practically from the day he was born. He had, furthermore, been dreadfully spoiled by his parents, but especially by his indulgent Mama, who'd lost several babies before and after producing him. Under her doting tutelage, the precocious boy had learned early how to wheedle his way out of a scolding with a show of penitence. So, too, had he learned how sweet words could melt away anger and clever phrases turn disapproval into laughter. He'd begun early practising these and the hundred other arts of which he was now the consummate master.

Small wonder it was so difficult to resist him when he was determined not to be resisted. Nature had given him both a fiendishly quick mind and a handsome face and form. Nurture had showed him how to use these to his advantage, and somehow along the way, self-discipline had never come into the picture.

Not that it was so terribly helpful to understand him better. What she learned about him only made her heart warm towards him in a way that was not at all sensible.

She was a greater fool than any of the Osbornes, certainly. They at least had stupidity as an excuse. Still, it was impossible to be unhappy now when he seemed so determined to make the ride a pleasant one, free of teasing innuendoes. He'd actually provided her an escape of sorts. No worrying, as she always did when she was with Lord Arden, about whether she was behaving too warmly or too coldly. Nor was there the guilt she always felt about allowing the marquess to court her when she was promised to another, or about building a friendship with his sister under the same false pretences. What would they think of her if they learned the truth?

"You're thinking unhappy thoughts," Basil chided, breaking in on her meditations, "which is most inconsiderate when I'm confiding my deepest secrets to you. Or is it the secrets that make you frown?"

"Oh. Not at all. I was only envying you your playmates," she improvised hastily. "We lived very quietly, you know, and I hadn't any."

"Then you saved yourself and your household a deal of trouble."

He went on to give examples. The Farrington children habitually spent part of the summer at Hartleigh Hall, where Jessica had early cultivated the disagreeable habit of tagging after the boys.

"One day she annoyed Will so, he tied her to a tree, but not nearly well enough. The little thing—and she was barely six years old—got herself free, then proceeded to stumble into a ditch. Nothing daunted, the child stumbled her way out again and marched home, muddy and bruised. She swore up and down she'd been kidnapped by gypsies. Jess would never tattle, one must say that for her. Even so, Will earned himself a flogging, and I—at my advanced age—was kept indoors for a week and required to copy pages and pages of dreary sermons."

"I daresay you copied them beautifully and learned a great deal from the experience."

"And I can tell by the look on your face you think I'd have been better for a flogging. Yet it never did Will any good, did it? He tried, in fact, to drown her not long after. Shall I show you the melancholy scene of his attempted crime?"

Without waiting for an answer, he led her deeper into the wood through such a maze of paths that she lost her bearings completely. Not that she was capable of noting the direction they took. Basil kept up a stream of nonsense as they proceeded, making such a tragicomedy of his anecdote that all she could do was follow him blindly, laughing all the way, until they reached the famous stream.

"We'd better walk the rest of the way," he told her. "The going is treacherous on horseback. At any rate, the beasts deserve a respite, and I'm thirsty."

He helped her dismount, and his touch at her waist sent a tremour through her. Rather unsteadily, she followed him to a curve of the bank where large rocks made a safe and comfortable sitting.

"A childhood paradise," he said, after they'd refreshed themselves and leaned back to relax upon the great, smooth stones.

"Or even an adult one," she agreed. "It's so beautiful and cool here."

"Yes, it is. My cousin is a lucky man. There was a time I thought he'd never live to enjoy it, and it would all be mine. He was involved in some rather dangerous intelligence work during the war, you know," he explained.

"As were you. And you both survived."

"Yes. What wonders we Trevelyans are." He appeared lost in thought, and not very pleasant thought at that. His features hardened slightly, and his amber eyes were shadowed.

"You didn't care for that work at all, did you?" she asked, after a bit.

"No. I hated it."

"Did your cousin feel the same?"

"He loved it—or at least the accomplishment. No one can like what he sees along the way. Of course, the accommodations are not always what they should be. He spent time in prison, and I soon learned to inspect my bed and boots before getting into them. When one is surrounded by unreliable allies, snakes and scorpions tend to turn up at the oddest times. At any rate, Edward knew what he was getting into and was prepared to make the necessary sacrifices. I'm not nearly so noble. I was sent away, you know, because—well, you must know that, too, by now. Ironic, isn't it? To be banished in disgrace, and then to find myself playing the hero. Hardly my style."

He'd never before discussed his exile, and the trace of bitterness in his tone surprised her. This wasn't the careless, complacent man she thought she knew.

"Yet you were—are—a hero," she answered carefully.

"In spite of myself." He tossed a pebble into the water. "I wonder," he said, after a moment, "what we'd become if we could do exactly as we wished."

"We should be in a sort of anarchy, of course. At least, that's what my governess always said."

"Why do I think, Alexandra, that you put little stock in

what your governess said?" He tossed another pebble into the stream and turned to smile at her.

The smile was sunshine, breaking through the gloom that had clouded his handsome face. She smiled back, happy that she'd helped dispel his somber mood.

"Because," she answered lightly, "you've already discovered what an undutiful daughter I am."

"And if you could do as you wished? If there was no Randolph hovering like a tiresome ghost in the background?"

She closed her eyes briefly to shut out his smiling, sunlit face so that she could conjure up an acceptable response. "It would be pleasant to have a Season," she answered, opening them again. "I had one, but Mama was always nagging. Then she was so ill towards the end of it, and even back then, there was the Randolph ghost in the background. I'd like to be free to enjoy myself this time and make friends with aged debutantes like myself—"

"And flirt with all the gentlemen?"

She grinned. "Well, not *all*. That would be selfish, and then I shouldn't have any women friends, should I?"

"I'd like to see that," was the surprising answer. "I'd like to see you at all the balls and routs, leaving dozens of broken hearts strewn in your wake. Including Will's. For that I'd even volunteer my own. The one you say I haven't got. You know, the little hard one. Looks something like this." He held up a pebble in illustration, then flung it carelessly over his shoulder.

"And is that what you'd like me to do with it?"

"With Will's, rather. Mine—"

Basil broke off abruptly. His thoughts were tending in a rather disconcerting direction, as they had earlier, and he wondered at it. But then, just look at her. She was so beautiful that it took one's breath away to gaze at her. She was always beautiful, even in those black rags she'd worn in Albania, but now her beauty was more than flesh and blood could bear. The ruby habit seemed to shimmer in the sunlight with every graceful movement of that slim, provocative body. A glass of exquisite wine, he thought, from which he longed to sip. Fortunately, he had sufficient self-control not to say so aloud. To anyone else he *would* have said it. He couldn't understand what made her different, or why that difference made him hold his tongue. Perhaps, right now he'd rather not understand.

Looking into her eyes was like gazing into a quiet forest, a place of refuge, and her low, husky voice was a cool, soothing stream, murmuring beside him. Meanwhile, this actually was a cool, shaded place by a clear, sparkling stream; and it *was* a sort of refuge. She was close by with no Will, no Randolph, no irascible Papa, nor watchful relatives of his own to interfere.

He even wished, for one dreadful moment, that it could always be so, and that was the oddest thought of all. He wanted her. His desire hadn't abated in all this time. Nor was there any more prospect of that desire being assuaged than there'd ever been. In spite of all that, he felt peaceful and contented.

She'd shunned him, and he hadn't liked it. Now he was shunned no longer, and idiotically happy . . . So relieved, in fact, that though he wanted her no whit less than he'd ever done since he met her, he forebore to act. And that was something. That was rather an immense something. But he couldn't think about it now. Later, perhaps, when those cool green eyes didn't confuse him so. At the moment, they were gazing at him inquiringly. He wondered how long he'd been staring at her, speechless.

He gave her a rueful grin. "See? You've only to mention a Season, and I immediately begin cudgelling my brains how to get you one. In fact, I wonder what the matter is. Surely my aunt would pay your Papa's debt."

"She tried to pay Mr. Burnham directly, she told me. And he declined to accept. Most indignantly declined, she says. Not," she added hurriedly, "that she *ought*—"

"Aunt Clem is never troubled by 'ought' or 'ought not.'

A trait that runs in the family, as you may have noticed. At any rate, she has no children of her own. Edward has always been a prodigy of virtue. Even I, despite every evidence to the contrary for over thirty years, have managed to get my own affairs in order. So you must be her offspring now. But it does puzzle me why there's only Will here courting you, instead of a few dozen competing for your attention."

Her face reddened. "You make me feel like the estate of a bankrupt to be auctioned off to the highest bidder."

"Why?"

"Because that's what I am." Though she spoke quietly there was suppressed emotion in her tone. He wasn't altogether surprised at what followed. "My father hasn't a farthing to call his own, and I'm his only asset. One way or another I'm to be used to pay his debt. If I'm not the commodity he offers in trade to the Burnhams, then I must be the means of getting them compensation." She shook her head then, as though to toss off what troubled her. "I'm sorry," she said. "I make it sound like a melodrama."

"You're stating the facts," he answered gently. "And the main fact is that whoever does pacify the Burnhams for your Papa will have a hold on you all the rest of your life, and the prospect appalls you."

She looked at him in astonishment.

"I understand you better than you think. And now," he went on, with a teasing smile, "you've as much as told me that Will hasn't won your heart, I'm more put out with my aunt than ever."

The faint rose of her cheeks deepened, telling him that she knew what she'd inadvertently confessed. Feeling absurdly relieved, he went on. "Since she's made such a mull of the business, perhaps I should step in and see what can be done to mend it."

"If you recall, you stepped in once already—"

"And must have accomplished something, for you aren't married to Randolph yet, are you?"

"No, I'm not, and it was very kind of you. If I didn't thank you before, I do thank you now. I do appreciate it," was her rather flustered reply.

"You needn't thank me. I might have done better, I suppose. Only I must confess I couldn't think of anything to improve upon our plan."

He could, of course, think of any number of improvements now, such as carrying her off somewhere out of Will's reach, out of everyone's reach. He could also . . . As the notion came to him, he crushed it. Momentary madness, brought on, no doubt, by the hope that flickered in her eyes.

"Well, it wants some thought, and I'm sure we've missed our tea. We'd better get back before they call in Bow Street."

He rose and offered his hand to help her up. He was alarmed to see that hand was shaking, but she didn't appear to notice as, rather absentmindedly, she let him help her to her feet.

He didn't let go, and she seemed oblivious to that as well, for her hand remained in his as he led her back to the horses. Though he'd much rather hold on to her in quite a different way, there was something so confiding in the simple gesture that he felt a rush of protectiveness towards her. Thus for the second—or perhaps hundredth—time that day, he forebore to act on his baser inclinations. If this set off any more alarm bells in his head, he decided to think about that later also.

The horses were now allowed to quench their thirst. He stood with her, quietly waiting as they did so. It was only when he'd helped her back upon her mount that he spoke again.

"How pleasant this has been. We haven't quarrelled once. I can't think how we've managed it."

"We've let our surroundings work their good upon us, I think. But I wouldn't worry overmuch about it. Once free of Nature's calming influence, I daresay we'll find something to dispute soon enough."

"I suspect you're right," he answered. It occurred to him that perhaps their relationship was a good deal safer when they *did* quarrel.

They returned to an anxious household. At Will's instigation, Edward had ordered horses saddled preparatory to searching for the missing pair. However, if he had it in mind to tax his cousin with keeping Miss Ashmore out so long, his wife's nudge must have distracted him. No one else scolded either, and Lord Arden could hardly make a scene. He had perforce to content himself with getting back into Miss Ashmore's good graces, while imagining divers hideous tortures to which Basil should be subjected if this were a more reasonable world—like that, for instance, in which the first Duke of Thorne had existed some centuries before.

Will soon found that he had best keep his mind entirely upon the former object, as Miss Ashmore's attention was not easily held. She was quite preoccupied and sometimes had to be asked the same question twice to be persuaded to answer at all. This circumstance was not encouraging. Lord Arden began to hate Basil desperately and the Osborne twins even more. Hadn't they sinned twice, after all: once in keeping him from Miss Ashmore, and again in boring him to distraction? Lord Arden began to consider the ugly possibility that he'd permanently alienated his Intended.

Fortunately for his lordship's spirits, which were sinking at an alarming rate, the group from Hartleigh Hall was engaged to dine that evening at Netherstone, home of Lord and Lady Dessing. In the course of that dinner, Miss Ashmore's behaviour gradually began to change.

She was less abstracted than she'd been. He had the good fortune to be seated at her left, a species of miracle, considering there were thirty at table. Will made the most of that advantage and he was soon rewarded with both smiles and humourous sallies from those sweetest of all lips.

He was also relieved to see that Trev was his usual self, flirting with all the females of the company by turns. He'd start on one and, as soon as that feminine heart was reduced to liquid state, would proceed on to the next. As there were at least half a dozen untried hearts to be worked upon, Basil was busy the entire evening.

When the gentlemen had consumed large quantities of port, they rejoined the ladies, and the marquess saw that Basil had reserved Lady Honoria Crofton-Ash, Dessing's daughter, for last. Well, if he could coax anything remotely resembling a natural smile onto the frigid countenance of that glacier-like creature, more power to him. Lord Arden did not believe Lady Honoria worth the effort. Priggish and haughty, entirely caught up in her own consequence, she held no charm for him, handsome as she was . . . and no charm, either, he suspected, for anyone else. After all, she'd be embarking upon her fifth Season in the spring, and for all her looks and all her Papa's money and consequence, she hadn't managed to find a husband.

At any rate, Basil's behaviour this evening showed that there was nothing to be concerned about there. He'd taken Miss Ashmore off this afternoon only to be provoking, and to prove what a prodigiously charming fellow he was—as he must demonstrate to every female in the county, apparently.

Let him be charming, the marquess thought as Miss Ashmore, who'd also glanced at the pair talking quietly in a corner of the room, turned back to him with a dazzling smile. Tonight Lord Arden did not envy the all-conquering Mr. Trevelyan his conquests. Not in the least.

= 11 =

Having, apparently, Learned His Lesson, the marquess was prompt to offer his services as driver the next morning when he learned that Miss Ashmore and Jess were going into the village.

His Intended did not seem to hear the offer, but Jess accepted readily, then went on to praise the local dress-maker who was taking in a gown for her. She complained about her London modiste whose careless work must now be repaired and ended by declaring she'd go to Madame Vernisse from now on. Look how beautifully she made Miss Ashmore's clothes.

Here Will interrupted with the avowal that whatever Miss Ashmore wore must be beautiful, since she adorned her attire, rather than the other way round.

Basil did not even look up from his plate, being busily engaged in creating a work of art therein. He moved a bit of egg here, a sliver of ham there, and was evidently so engrossed in this aesthetic endeavour that he forgot to put any of it in his mouth.

Doubtless he was fretting over his singular lack of success with Lady Honouria last night, for she'd been as stiff and proper with him at the end of the evening as she had at the start. Well, it was about time *somebody* found him resistible, Alexandra thought morosely. He'd tricked her into admitting she wasn't in love with Lord Arden, said he wanted to help her, then let the marquess monopolise her the entire evening. Mr. Trevelyan obviously couldn't be bothered with her problems when there was a roomful of ladies requiring his attention.

There was no help for her at all. It was either the marquess or Randolph, and no more delay, because Papa was coming—good grief!—this very afternoon. The recollection threw her into a panic, and she was so busy wracking her brains what to do next that she hardly noticed what she was doing now.

Which is to say she answered automatically what was said to her on the ride into the village and hadn't the presence of mind to think of a reasonable objection when Lord Arden insisted that Jess go on to the dressmaker by herself, to be met up with in another hour. Hardly had Jess been deposited at Mrs. Merrill's door and the horses put in motion again, when the marquess announced his intention of speaking to Sir Charles this very afternoon.

Alexandra's panic escalated. Stalling for time, she feigned bafflement about what the marquess might have to say to her father.

"Why, Miss Ashmore—Alexandra—surely it can come as no surprise to you," he said, with the tenderest of looks. "I'd thought I'd made my intentions perfectly plain. And I'd thought—or rather, *hoped*—that in some small way you might return those feelings."

She looked startled, and then she looked confused, and then she dropped her gaze to her hands which were tightly folded in her lap. She murmured that she had no business having feelings about anyone, as she was betrothed already. In halting sentences, she outlined the Burnham situation.

Lord Arden was, as she'd expected, speechless for a moment. She stole a glance at his face. His expression was composed, if rather tightly so, and the grey eyes seemed darker than usual, like cold slate, telling her he was angry. But whatever he felt, he held it in check, and only asked stiffly, "As to this betrothal—you say nothing of yourself, only of your Papa and this Mr. Burnham. Is it what you wish?"

With some hesitation, she admitted that it was not.

He seemed to relax a little. "Then dare I wonder whether there's any place for me in your wishes?"

She studied her hands again. She couldn't allow herself to think about . . . such things, she said. In fact—well, she'd been dishonest to keep this matter from others, and yet . . . She couldn't continue, being covered in maidenly confusion, but not so much so that she couldn't manage another peek at his face. He was mulling it over, she could tell, and must have come to a satisfactory conclusion, for very soon he was smiling again, and the warm light was back in his eyes.

"It seems to me," he said, "that if you had told me from the first, you would have been saying there was no hope for me at all. But as you didn't—well, perhaps it was because you weren't wholly indifferent to me. Or do I presume too much?"

"It's quite impossible, my lord, to be indifferent to you— as no doubt scores of other ladies have demonstrated. Still, I suppose I should have told you. And yet," she looked up to meet his gaze—"it didn't seem so important. How could I think that I, or my family matters, were of any interest to you? That would be assuming that out of all the women you know, I would be anything special to you."

He was stymied. She barely hinted—though she did so tantalisingly enough—at caring for him, which implied that she'd been playing fast and loose with him all this time. Then, in the same breath, she claimed to be the one led on. Damn Jessica for telling all those tales of his romantic conquests. They had made Miss Ashmore think he was only amusing himself, and now, though he'd courted the women all this time—two whole weeks, at least—it appeared he must begin all over again.

Meanwhile, she insisted she'd never believed his intentions were Serious. She couldn't be expected to make up her mind on the spot whether she meant to have him, as she'd never permitted herself to think of him in that way.

Besides which, she was already engaged, as she'd just told him, and she couldn't blame him in the least if he chose to forget this entire conversation. Certainly there were hundreds of women more deserving of the honour he so kindly offered.

The discussion went on for half an hour, until he finally convinced her that his suit was serious. As to speaking to her father, that—for now at least—was out of the question. Papa was sure to take alarm and ship her off to Yorkshire.

"He's very fixed on Randolph, and under great obligation to Mr. Burnham, and really—"

"And really," he interrupted impatiently, "his debts are the least of my concerns. The trivialities of the marriage settlement." He complained that she was bent on tormenting him.

She declared nothing could be farther from her mind, then looked as though she was about to weep. So he spoke more kindly, with a great deal of the sort of tender nonsense best calculated to soothe the tremulous flutterings of the fragile feminine heart.

Sir Charles arrived early in the afternoon in a state of high irritation. He had not liked to leave Westford so soon, as business with Henry Latham promised to be most satisfactory, but a letter from George Burnham had come to him there that drove everything else out of his head.

Nearly two days' journey in hot weather had only exacerbated his foul mood. Even Randolph had been provoking. The baronet had begun to speak of the Peloponnesian War, thinking to while away the weary hours with talk on Randolph's favorite subject, and got for his pains only a great, agonised groan.

The younger generation was going to the devil, and that was the long and short of it. His daughter was scheming with Clementina's nephew to foist this ridiculous secret betrothal nonsense upon her long-suffering Papa. Even Randolph—always such a steady chap—was in a fit of the dismals from the moment they left Westford. Well, Sir Charles would see about him, later. Right now, he had a few choice words for Clementina.

He could not say those words immediately, however, having only just arrived and been greeted by his host and hostess. Their warm welcome, along with the army of servants who appeared immediately to see to his comfort, the graciously appointed rooms allotted him, a hot bath, and a generous tray of refreshments provided for his delectation, helped control his impatience.

Nonetheless, he was determined to be in a temper, and when some hours later he was finally ushered into Lady Bertram's presence, he burst out without preamble, "I will not have it, Clementina!"

The countess sat perfectly straight in her chair and eyed him coldly as though he were a particularly hideous species of toad, then said with frigid composure, "Indeed?"

"How dare you?" he went on, undaunted by her haughty stare. "How dare you connive behind my back? How dare you attempt to bribe George Burnham?"

"Oh, do stop shouting, Charles. You'll have all the servants huddling by the door."

"I don't care a fiddle about the servants—"

"And *I* don't care to be shouted at. If you cannot behave yourself, you might as well leave." She gave him a dismissive wave.

"You needn't put on your high and mighty airs with me, Clementina," he retorted, but more quietly. "Though it's of a perfect piece with your interfering arrogance. You tried to bribe George Burnham. There's no use denying it."

"I," said Lady Bertram, with awful dignity, "deny nothing."

"Then you did try!"

"You understand nothing. I did not attempt to bribe George Burnham. I offered to pay your debt to him—"

"To prevent the marriage."

"To pay the debt. I do not see what marriage has to do

with it. A financial debt is one thing; a marriage is another. You seem to confuse the two."

"Never mind what confuses me. You had no business."

The countess maintained that she had every sort of business since her goddaughter was somehow mixed into his business affairs. "As she did not create your financial difficulties, I do not see why she is required to solve them for you."

There was obvious truth in what Lady Bertram said, and that truth rather piqued his conscience than otherwise. Therefore, Sir Charles grew more enraged. "But you could see your way well enough to plotting against me, could you not? You and your scheming nephew."

"I collect you are referring to Basil."

"Of course I'm referring to Basil."

"Then why do you come and pick a quarrel with me? If Basil has offended you, it is Basil you should speak with."

Sir Charles's head was beginning to ache. The woman jumped about from one topic to the next with no logic whatsoever. Sir Charles hated illogic. He hated non sequiturs, and at the moment, he was so little fond of Lady Bertram that he would have liked to choke her. He wondered now why he had bothered to confront her in the first place. He should have known he'd get nowhere. Still, George Burnham's letter had wounded his pride, and Sir Charles wanted to take it out on somebody. He glared at the countess, but forced himself into some semblance of composure.

"That I will do—in good time—but first I wanted you to understand that I won't have you interfering in my affairs—"

"Where they concern my goddaughter, I cannot help but interfere. I hold it as a debt to Juliet."

"Was it part of that debt to send your nephew to connive with my daughter?"

"I cannot allow you to speak so when he is not here to defend himself." She gestured towards the bell rope. "Ring for a servant, Charles, and we shall send for Basil—and for Alexandra, too. If she has been conniving with him, then let her answer for herself."

Sir Charles rang, grumbling as he did so, and for several minutes after as they waited. Lady Bertram paid no heed to his ill-natured mutterings. She sat, straight as a ramrod, rigidly calm.

At last, the two connivers entered the room. Alexandra, who hadn't seen her Papa until now, gave him an affectionate peck on the cheek.

Angrily he waved her away. "None of your coaxing arts, Miss," he growled. "I've had enough of them."

He then launched into a tirade about make-believe fiancés, bribery of friends, and betrayal of Randolph, who was supposedly in the process of breaking his heart. No one but Lady Bertram noticed the flicker of interest in Basil's eyes as this last piece of information was communicated. Meanwhile, the baronet went on to his primary grievance— and here he took a letter out of his pocket—the very upsetting words he'd had from his friend, George Burnham.

"Well, Basil," said Lady Bertram when the baronet paused for breath. "What have you to say to that?"

"I hardly know what to say, Aunt. There's so much of it." He was leaning against the door frame, completely at his ease, wearing his most seraphic expression.

Miss Ashmore, he noticed, looked panicked, and well she should. If her Papa was not quickly brought under control, she'd be whisked off to Yorkshire and married to the wool merchant's son before the week was out.

It would be best if she were married and kept far away, beyond his reach. She was spoiling his fun. Hadn't she disrupted his entertainment last night? And he'd been so determined to find pleasure in other company, had so looked forward to it.

There was the Honourable Miss Sheldon, who'd refused to speak to him in the old days, and Miss Carstone. Even the haughty Honoria had endured a conversation, and her Mama had positively beamed upon him. Yet, they might have been a pack of murdering Hindoos for all the joy he had of them.

Not that he needed to wonder why there should be so little joy in it. The cause was here before him, artful creature that she was. Well then, if she was so artful, let her get herself out of this fix.

He glanced towards her then, their eyes met, and he found himself saying, "Of course, as to the fiancé part of your question, the answer is plain enough. She promised herself to me six years ago, and I mean to hold her to that promise."

"You *what?*" Sir Charles cried.

"I mean to—"

"What kind of fool do you take me for? I know as well as everyone else in this room that was a great piece of nonsense you concocted."

"Are you calling me a liar, sir?" Basil asked quietly.

Alexandra, who'd apparently been struck mute by the previous exchange, now found her tongue. "No, he isn't." She turned to her father. "You know you aren't saying any such thing, Papa."

"I most certainly am. And if this young blackguard wishes to name his seconds—"

"Oh, do be quiet, Charles. He wishes nothing of the sort. But you can hardly expect my nephew to stand quietly by as you denigrate his"—the countess appeared to have got something stuck in her throat, but she quickly recovered—"his tender feelings for your daughter."

"That's it precisely, Aunt. My tender feelings." He glanced again at Alexandra, expecting her to take the cue.

Instead, she crossed the room to Basil's side. "You can't get at me through my Papa, Basil," she said, with a look of deepest pity. "I told you it was a mistake." She turned to her father. "It's as you predicted, Papa."

"What is?" asked the now-bewildered baronet.

"Why, it was only romantic infatuation—as you said—and now—"

"And now," Basil interposed, beginning to grow very angry, "you're infatuated with someone else and mean to throw me over. I should have known I couldn't compete with a marquess."

"A what? What's going on here? Clementina, they're at it again, and I hold you responsible."

"On the contrary," the countess remarked serenely, "they are at each other. But really, Basil, you needn't sulk. After all, it is a compliment to be jilted in favour of a marquess. A future duke, actually."

"Will someone please speak rationally and logically? Because if they do not, I warn you, Alexandra, you'll be out of this house and on your way to Yorkshire in the next ten minutes."

"The situation is quite simple, Charles. Lord Arden, Thorne's heir, has evidently succeeded in engaging your daughter's affections."

"But the wretched girl is engaged already. Twice, it seems, if I am to believe all this faradiddle about tender feelings."

"That is neither here nor there. To expect her to marry a wool merchant's son or my black sheep of a nephew"—the nephew, at the moment, had a rather black look about him, indeed—"when the future Duke of Thorne wishes to make her his wife, is perfectly absurd. It is the most illogical thing I have ever heard."

Sir Charles, whose head was now spinning, dropped into a chair. "Thorne?" he uttered faintly. Then he remembered the letter still clutched in his hand. "But what of this? What reply am I to make to this?"

Casting a warning look at Basil, Alexandra took the letter from her father. She read it through, quickly, frowning as she did so. "Why, this is infamous, Papa!" she exclaimed, when she was done. "See how the man insults you. And to go on at such length about injured friendship and in the next breath talk of the money, when he as much as says the money is nothing to him. Oh, Papa, no wonder you were so overset." She spoke with such tender compassion that even Basil half-believed her—for a moment.

"Well, it was most distressing. Especially when he knows I fully intended—but what reply can I make him now?"

"Why, that I'm to be mar—"

Basil hastily interrupted, "If it's as your daughter says, sir, then perhaps you should make no answer—not immediately. You'll want to frame a suitable reply, will you not?" he added, ignoring Miss Ashmore's look of outrage.

"Basil is right, Charles. The man has no choice but to be patient. And in a week or so, perhaps, you may answer him as coolly and logically as you like."

"Yes, Papa. You'll know exactly how to put him in his place—but later, when you're calmer."

He gazed for a moment at the three faces surrounding him, but all looked perfectly sincere—all seemed, suddenly, prodigious concerned with his peace of mind. He didn't trust any of them, and yet what could he do? A dukedom was nothing to sneeze at. With Thorne's patronage, a man might explore the globe for the rest of his life with never a care in the world. And if there were no dukedom, then Alexandra would marry Randolph.

Defeated for the moment, the baronet shrugged and agreed that George Burnham could wait. Exhausted with trying to distinguish between truth and humbug, he struggled up from the chair and out of the room.

"Well, what are you glaring at each other for?" Lady Bertram asked when the door had closed behind him. "You fuddled him well enough, between the two of you, and I should be deeply ashamed of you both if it had not been so very amusing. Well, well. Run along now, Alexandra. I wish to have a word with my nephew."

Alexandra ran along readily enough, not liking the expression on Mr. Trevelyan's face. Whatever was the matter with him? Was this how he meant to help, with that old betrothal farce that Papa plainly didn't believe for a moment? Thank heavens she hadn't counted on help from that quarter. Now what was she to do?

The amount George Burnham referred to in his letter wasn't the "thousand pounds or so" she'd heard Papa mention over the years. She'd read the words again and again, disbelieving her eyes, and hardly noticing the rest of the insulting missive. She couldn't understand how the amount had grown so. But then, what did Papa know of finance? Annuities and percents were as unfathomable to him as his beloved ancient inscriptions were to others. That was why he'd put everything in Mr. Burnham's hands. And how he'd tied the noose about her neck.

She'd have to marry Arden now—if he'd have her. If he wouldn't, Papa would simply shrug and take her away. She could appeal to Aunt Clem—but both conscience and pride recoiled at the idea of begging more help from her indulgent godmother.

Alexandra went to her room and tried to think. So many lies—to everyone—and matters only grew more muddled and horrible. Arden hadn't turned a hair when she'd mentioned Papa's debt—but what would he think now?

Did he want her badly enough to pay this outrageous marriage settlement? She didn't believe he truly loved her. He struck her less as a man in love than as one pursuing a prize.

Was that what offended her so? Though he said all the right words, she felt he could have been saying them to anybody. He didn't seem to know—or care—who she was.

Not, she reminded herself, that he'd necessarily *like* who she was: a manipulative, deceitful woman who was only using him to save herself from boring Randolph and his appalling sisters. She had no right to judge the marquess so harshly.

She'd have to think of some way to break the news about the money. That was sure to be awkward. She attempted to compose an appropriate speech, but her mind kept returning to one point in the previous conversation, when Basil had said he meant to have her. He'd sounded as though he *did* mean it, and her heart had thumped dreadfully, as it was thumping now. Oh, such a fool she was. What was the good of his saying it if he wasn't going to sound as though he meant it?

= 12 =

FOR THE NEXT two days, Basil kept well away from her, Aunt Clem having warned him, as she told Alexandra, "to keep his interfering self out of this business." It was most gratifying to see how well he obeyed his aunt, especially, Alexandra thought dismally, when Aunt Clem's orders so perfectly coincided with his own fickle inclinations.

Still, it was odd that he'd taken up with Randolph, of all people. Apparently determined to be Mr. Burnham's bosom bow, Basil stuck to the young scholar like glue, toured him about the estate, and spent hours talking with him. Randolph must have found these discussions uplifting, for he'd come to Hartleigh Hall in a state of tragic melancholy. Now, after only two days, he was actually grinning at the man he'd begged her to beware of.

Oh, well, Alexandra thought wearily, it was nothing to her. She had her hands full with Arden.

Today they were sharing a picnic lunch with the Osbornes and another group of neighbours. Determined to have her exclusive company, Lord Arden had borne her off to a spot a little distance from the others. There he treated her to such a series of compliments and affectionate hints and delicate renderings of life at Thornehill—as well as the rest of the Farrington estates, so numerous she couldn't keep them straight in her mind—that he gave her a splitting headache.

Remarking her pallor, he suggested a walk. The meal

had been laid out in a cool, shady grove, and he pointed to a path that followed alongside a sparkling stream.

"Hadn't we better invite the others?" she asked, as he helped her to her feet and drew her arm though his.

"Whatever for?"

She cast a furtive glance towards Basil, whose head was now bent very close to Hetty's simpering face. Any excuse Alexandra might have made died on her lips. Gripping the marquess's arm more firmly, she manufactured a shy smile.

That was answer enough for Will. He smiled down at her in a protective, proprietary sort of way, patted the slim fingers that lay on his sleeve, and bore her off towards the path.

No one appeared to take any alarm at their departure. Not Sir Charles, certainly, to whom it was comforting proof of the marquess's interest in his daughter. As Alexandra's own Papa did not object to the business, no one else felt required to do so, either.

No one, that is, but Basil, who took great exception to this impropriety. He wondered, as his hooded gaze followed the departing pair, what the devil Ashmore was thinking of to countenance it. It would have been easy enough to persuade Hetty to stroll in the same direction, but that was risky. Her Mama was bound to expect certain news at the conclusion of the exercise. Nor could Basil look with equanimity upon the prospect of stumbling, with witnesses, upon what was bound to be a compromising situation.

As the minutes ticked away, the danger of there being a compromising situation to witness increased. Still, if no one else cared, why should he? Consequently, between tormenting himself with imagining what was happening between the pair, and assuring himself of his perfect indifference to the lurid scenes presenting themselves to his imagination, he did not at first notice the parasol that tapped his arm. It tapped again, and a weary sigh floated down from somewhere above his head. He looked up to see

Lady Deverell gazing down at him in a very bored sort of way.

"Dear me, how tiresome I am, to be sure. You did not look to be asleep, Basil, and yet Harry is—" She pointed with her parasol to her husband, who appeared to be dozing, propped up against a tree. "And I had hoped to have your arm for a bit."

Basil, who'd been reclining upon a cushion Hetty had thoughtfully provided for him, scrambled to his feet, all gallantry. If he thought it odd that Maria, who considered sitting down upon her chaise longue a calisthenic exercise, wanted to take a walk, he was too polite to mention it.

"It would be an honour, my lady. I'm yours to be led wheresoever you wish."

Having been deserted by one swain, Hetty very sensibly turned her attention elsewhere. She had a riddle, she told Lady Tuttlehope, that she was sure even the clever Mr. Burnham couldn't solve. Lady Tuttlehope protested that this was impossible. Mr. Burnham made modest noises that it was not, and Lord Tuttlehope, greatly baffled, blinked in wonder as he watched his friend stroll away with Harry Deverell's wife.

"I felt so dull," was the viscountess's soft complaint. "And that little path by the stream seems pleasant, does it not?"

Agreeing that it seemed most pleasant, Basil bore her away in pursuit of the missing couple.

"It has rather more twists and turns than one would expect," she noted languidly, when they'd walked some moments in silence. "Why, here it branches off. Now I wonder—" She paused at a place where the trail divided into three narrow paths.

Although it was not one of the sites he'd shown Miss Ashmore, Basil knew the place well, having, in the past, coaxed more than one willing village maiden along the more private of these ways. Yet, strangely enough, it was in this very direction that he proposed they proceed.

"Oh, well, I suppose you know best, my dear. And yet how easy for one to become lost—it does grow rather a wilderness, does it not? I do hope that Will has not lost his way."

"Highly unlikely," was the stiff reply. "He knows the place as well as I do."

"Does he? Then I daresay he will not cause Miss Ashmore to overexert herself."

"I daresay."

It appeared that Lord Arden must have expected exertion of some sort, for as the path turned and branched off once again they came upon a pretty, sheltered spot, and upon the marquess with his arms wrapped around Miss Ashmore, treating her to a very interesting sort of exercise, indeed.

Being fully occupied, the pair were unaware they were observed, though Basil was instantly prepared to bring that matter forcibly to their attention. He was, in fact, about to rush forward and knock his lordship to the ground when he felt a surprisingly firm grip on his arm, and found himself being tugged backwards, out of sight.

"Scenes," her ladyship whispered, as he opened his mouth to object, "are so very fatiguing." She went on, in more carrying tones than normal, to rhapsodise in her usual weary way about the attractiveness of the spot. "Yes, a charming place, my love. I daresay Mr. Wordsworth would be moved to compose any number of odes upon it— with a perfectly exhausting number of stanzas." As she spoke, she led Basil forward again. "But you know, these noisy brooks do grow rather wearisome to the head after a time."

He hardly knew what he answered—some incoherent inanity. For all his outward composure, Basil was in a murderous rage, a condition not conducing to clever repartee. He thought of another stream and another private spot, and of how careful he'd been not to offend Miss Ashmore by making improper advances. Now that designing female was locked in an embrace with a man she'd admitted she didn't love. With a man, for heaven's sake, who had a set of twins in his keeping in London. It would serve her right to be shackled all her days to that monster of depravity.

If he did not stop to recall that Will had done little worse in his lifetime than he had himself, it was perhaps because Basil was not quite himself at the moment. How else explain that he, who'd always thought it great sport to steal kisses as often as he could, should now be filled with moral outrage that another gentleman did so? But it was Miss Ashmore from whom the kiss was stolen, and that, somehow, turned everything upside down.

Not that he could tell, really, what was upside down or right side up, for he was nearly choked with fury. He was, in fact, vowing to himself that as soon as the ladies could be removed from the vicinity, he would tear the marquess limb from limb. And as to *her* . . . There was a warning pressure on his arm, and he tried to collect himself. They were once again in view of the couple, now walking innocently towards them.

Miss Ashmore, who'd apparently found it unnecessary to lean upon her escort's arm, hurried towards Lady Deverell, and greeted her with a rather set smile.

"It seems," she said, in a voice as tight as her smile, "that Lord Arden has lost his way—"

"Has he, my love? Well, that is what we thought, is it not, Basil?" Without waiting for his reply, the viscountess remarked what a confusing sort of maze it was, and how it was no wonder Will went astray. "Yes, very likely, my dear," she told Will as she absently let go of Basil's arm to take that of the marquess. "You confused the spot with that lovely little wood you told me of, at the edges of your place in Scotland."

The way his lordship leered at Miss Ashmore as he accepted this excuse could not be agreeable to certain of the company. Miss Ashmore, however, resolutely turned her head . . . only to confront a face that appeared to be carved in stone. Lady Deverell having laid claim to the marquess, Alexandra had no choice but to take the arm Basil stiffly proffered her.

She no sooner touched his sleeve than she was acutely aware of the taut strength beneath her fingers. A tear pricked her eye, and she struggled to fight it back. It was unfair. Will's kiss had left her profoundly unmoved, and now . . . oh, Lord, she had only to touch Basil's coatsleeve and she was all atremble inside. It was unfair and cruel.

And he was cruel as well, hurrying her along ahead of the other two and acting so cold and silent just when she most needed him to tease her out of her misery. If only he'd say something provoking to make her forget Will's embrace and the self-loathing she'd felt in permitting it. She'd felt like a Cyprian, selling herself to a man she didn't, *couldn't* love. When it had come to the point, when she'd heard the voices and known that she had only to stay in his arms a moment longer, and all her problems would be solved . . . she couldn't do it. It had only wanted a moment. They'd have been caught, and Papa would have made her marry the man who'd compromised her. But what had she done? Jerked herself away—because all she could think of was Basil seeing her in another man's arms.

As if he cared. He was only in a hurry to get back to Hetty and her sisters. Well, who told him to leave them in the first place?

"My apologies," Basil said in a harsh undertone, "for interrupting your tête-à-tête."

He'd broken in upon what was rapidly becoming a most satisfying wallow in self-pity. She managed to invent a cold retort, but his accusing tone had made her throat ache and her eyes fill with tears. To her horror, she heard her voice quavering as she answered, "Pray don't tax yourself with it, sir. I daresay his lordship makes his own opportunities for private conversation."

The tremulous sound made Basil look at her sharply, just as one treacherous tear stole down her cheek. He'd been about to say something brutal, but now found that he couldn't. A tear. He'd tasted a tear once before, eons ago, it seemed. It hadn't then, as it did now—so hurriedly brushed away—aroused in him this frenzy of emotions: pain, rage, sorrow, shame, and he didn't know what else.

He wanted to pull her into his arms, pull her close to him, as though that would end the turmoil within him—or at least punish her for causing it. She'd driven him to this: made him mad with jealousy and then in the next instant broke his heart in a thousand pieces when she shed a tear.

Mad with jealousy? Heart in a thousand pieces? Good heavens! That was what one *said* to women. It wasn't what one *felt*.

Mr. Trevelyan was not a stupid man. He knew himself very well. He knew, therefore, that whatever his previous opinions regarding what one said and what one felt, Reality was presenting him with a very different state of affairs. He had better take his hint from Reality for now and work out his opinions on the matter later.

"I'm sorry," he said quickly. "I was only teasing, and had no business—oh, for heaven's sake, Alexandra." Another tear was trembling on her long, black lashes. "Please don't cry. Not about *him*." He quickened his pace to draw her still further ahead of Will and Maria, then took out his handkerchief, which he surreptitiously gave her.

"I was not crying," she insisted, though she did wipe her eyes hurriedly before returning the linen square to him.

"No, of course you weren't," he agreed. Tearing the marquess limb from limb was too kind by half. If that clumsy brute had in any way abused her . . . but his voice was light enough as he went on. "And so, of course I needn't worry that the others might notice it and wonder what's been going on. Or if they do," he added, "they're bound to think it's my fault and naturally I'm quite used to being scolded. I daresay Edward will horsewhip me, but don't trouble yourself about it. Really, don't."

In this wise he got her to smile and compose herself, so that when the four wanderers rejoined the rest of the party, not a murmur was made regarding their wanderings.

Lord Hartleigh was a cultured man and had, in addition to an excellent art collection, a well-stocked library. It was to this place that Sir Charles would repair as soon as he'd discharged his little social duties. The earl had not only invited him to make himself at home there, but had considerately pointed out those parts of the collection in which his guest would have the greatest interest.

It was to this, his favourite refuge, that Alexandra accompanied her father after they returned from the picnic. He was so eager to get back to the old Stuart and Revett volume, *The Antiquities of Athens*, with its beautiful engravings, that he forgot to ask his daughter whether Lord Arden had shown any signs of coming to the point during their stroll.

Spared having to tell her Papa more lies, Alexandra breathed a sigh of relief as she stepped over the threshold. Closing the door behind her, she turned . . . and nearly collided with Mr. Trevelyan.

"Good heavens, I didn't know you were there. How quietly you come upon one." Like a cat, she thought. Backing away, she found herself flat up against the door.

He only stared at her in a considering sort of way that made her acutely uncomfortable. She took a step to the side to put a little distance between them. He copied her motion.

"Very funny," she muttered. "Now if you'd please get out of the way."

"And if I don't please?" His voice was soft and beckoning, and he was close, much too close. But with a grandfather clock a few inches away on one side, and a rather heavy table on the other, she couldn't continue to sidle against the wall. Besides, it wasn't dignified. She was about to push past him when his hands abruptly came to rest upon the wall on either side of her, blocking her escape. He was so very close that she could feel his breath on her face. Directly in her line of vision was his mouth. Feeling her cheeks grow exceedingly warm, she dropped her eyes to his neckcloth.

"Stop it!" she hissed.

He only bent closer, his mouth inches from hers. "Or what, my love? You'll scream for your Papa? I don't think so." His lips brushed hers softly, and her own parted helplessly. She found herself crushed between him and the wall—which was fortunate, for her knees immediately buckled, and it was most unlikely she could have stood up under her own power.

Even as he kissed her he knew it was exactly the wrong thing to do. He told himself, as he tasted her soft, sweet lips, that he must leave her—immediately. Then he felt her hands creep up to his chest, as though she'd push him away. Except that she didn't. Her hands rested there a moment—she must feel his heart hammering—before proceeding, hesitantly, up to his neck. The light touch upon his skin sent a tiny, delicious chill running down his spine to the very tips of his toes.

He shivered slightly and crushed her close to him, as he'd wanted to do all these long weeks. In a moment, he promised himself, he'd stop. At any rate, she'd *make* him stop, but she only gave a faint, surprised gasp, and melted against him. His mind grew very hazy, as though a thick fog was enveloping his brain. All that remained was sensation: her skin was like silk, and the curves of her lithe body molded naturally to his own, as though she were a part of him long missing.

His lips brushed her ear, then moved to tickle the nape of her neck with soft kisses that made her tremble, but still she made no struggle. When his tongue invaded her mouth, her fingers only pressed his shoulders more tightly, as though she felt the same hunger he did. The fog thickened. It was such a warm, inviting sort of fog, and he was such a lazy, unreliable vessel that he gave himself up for lost, content to drown where he was because she was in his arms, and that was all that mattered.

The lost Trevelyan vessel might have drifted onto treacherous waters, but something awakened him to his peril. At the very edge of his consciousness, a warning bell seemed to go off. Not struggling. And where were they? In a hallway. A hallway!

He drew a ragged breath. "Alexandra, you must make me stop."

She pulled back from him a little to gaze into his eyes. In the next instant, she was smiling in the most provocative way, as her hands dropped to his coat, which she methodically began to unbutton.

"Alexandra," he gasped. "Stop it!"

She looked up at him innocently. "Or what? You'll scream for Papa? I don't think so."

Though he felt like screaming, he didn't. Instead, his hand closed firmly over hers. Damn! What on earth was wrong with him? He endeavoured to summon up some dignity. "What do you think you're doing, you wicked, wretched girl?"

She looked at his rumpled cravat and at his creased shirt and at his unbuttoned coat and answered, "Isn't that what I was supposed to do?"

"Good God, no—oh, damn it all—" He pulled her along, down the hallway and into the music room. When he'd shut the door, he burst out—though he kept his voice low—"Are you mad? In the *hall?* Where the servants—"

"Well, you seemed to think it all right—"

"It is not all right to undress me in public. Who ever taught you such things? Don't tell me that sneaking Farrington—"

"No," she answered indignantly. "Nobody taught me. I deduced it. From the general to the specific, you know."

"From the what?"

The words made him feel warm, dangerously warm, again. Her hand was still in his, and he wanted that slender, provocative body close again. Her curls, in great disorder now, fell about her face, and he wanted, so much, to disorder her a great deal more. That was insane. No, it wasn't. He was lost, quite lost, and there was no point pretending that anything else—his freedom, the pleasures he'd fantasised about for three years—mattered. There was no peace for him without her. But what could he say? What would she believe, knowing him as she did?

While he struggled to collect his scattered wits, she'd evidently gathered hers. She was replying, and quite composedly, too, "Well, there you were, you know, set on amusing yourself with me again. So I thought I'd use the opportunity."

"Use the opportunity?" he echoed stupidly, wondering at the icy chill that suddenly replaced all that cozy warmth.

"Why, yes. For practice." Smoothly she disengaged her hand from his. She smiled—the same pitying smile she'd given him a few days ago, when they'd put on that performance for her father. "For my husband," she explained. Then she laughed . . . and left him.

As he stared after her at the empty doorway, a great clattering started up in his brain. She could not mean, really—not another man tasting those kisses, touching her. No, it was impossible. It was wicked, and *cruel*. Practising for her husband—on *him*—he'd kill her. No, he'd teach her a lesson she wouldn't soon forget—but there was Randolph, and Arden, and a thousand other men. She couldn't be so stupid, to throw herself away—and yet she knew him too well—amusing himself. But he wasn't. He *wasn't*. Through it all, as his brain leapt from one half notion to the next, he could still feel her touch, still feel the aching need that had gripped him as her fingers tugged at the buttons of his coat.

He stood there, frozen, for what seemed like hours, his mind churning. Then, drawing a deep breath to steady himself, he rebuttoned his coat and left the room.

= 13 =

ALEXANDRA WAS CROUCHED down outside the library door when she heard footsteps. Hastily she rose, preparing a plausible explanation for crawling about on the carpet. Oh, Lord. It was him, again. Her pulse began to race. In answer to his quizzical look, she said, "I was looking for my hairpins."

He stared at her touselled curls, then down at the carpet and back at her hair. "I'll help you," he said quietly.

"No—"

But he'd already bent to search and was quickly gathering the stray pins. "It wouldn't do for the servants to find them." He straightened and dropped them into her outstretched palm.

"I'm leaving," he said.

"Oh."

"To London."

"Well."

"It's what I meant to tell you before—" He nodded towards her hand, in which the pins were clutched.

She hardly noticed that they were digging into her flesh, for she felt ill suddenly, and frightened. Going away . . . abandoning her . . . to Will. Oh, why hadn't she kept her spiteful mouth shut? Why had she tried to best him at his own game? That disgraceful scene a few minutes ago had been as much her fault as his. She should never have let it go so far—should have stopped it at the outset. But he had only to touch her, and she went to him, like one mesmerised. It was better this way, she told herself, fighting down the panic. Better he should go away.

"I see. Well, then, good-bye, Mr. Trevelyan."

"You might at least bid me to the devil by my given name, and it isn't Randolph."

She shifted the hairpins from her right hand to her left and put out the empty hand. "Good-bye, Basil."

Instead of shaking her hand, he raised it to his lips and dropped a kiss on her palm. "Good-bye, Miss Ashmore," he whispered. Then he was gone.

Mr. Trevelyan for once was as good as his word. He left Hartleigh Hall a little before dinnertime, despite his family's strenuous objections to his travelling at night. Alexandra did not raise any objections, having gone to her room with a headache.

It must have been an excessively painful one, because she wept half the night and only fell asleep when she was too tired to sob any more. The few hours' rest was sufficient, apparently, for no sooner did she open her eyes the next morning than her tears fell afresh. This would never do, she scolded herself. It was stupid to weep over him. She had, it appeared, fallen in love with him, as had, she was sure, hundreds of other women. She should, therefore, be thankful she hadn't got into worse trouble. If they'd been in a more private place yesterday, he might easily have seduced her. She had absolutely no self-control when it came to him, and she could hardly trust him to take care what he did.

Nor could she expect, if he did ruin her, that he'd marry her willingly, or attempt to change his behaviour thereafter. Because she did love him, his inevitable infidelities would humiliate and grieve her all the rest of her life. Will's infidelities, on the other hand, she could look upon with equanimity: his mistresses would only relieve her of his company.

Having disposed of matters of the heart to her morose

and cynical satisfaction, she went on to matters of business, i.e., Papa's radically increased debt. She'd been reluctant to confide the news to her godmother. It had troubled her when Aunt Clem tried to pay George Burnham before—and look how it had infuriated Papa. Besides, no one should pay it. The amount was outrageous. Papa couldn't possibly have run up such a sum unless he kept a dozen mistresses and spent the remainder of his time in gambling hells. Someone should investigate. But if it were Aunt Clem, Papa was bound to resent the meddling in his affairs, take three temper fits at once, and hustle his daughter off to Yorkshire before she could blink.

The more she thought of it, the more obvious it became that the only person who could investigate without enraging Papa was her future husband. The Duke of Thorne's lawyers would insist on it, anyhow, and George Burnham would probably find himself swatted down like a pesky fly. Well, then. That was that.

Having mentally settled all that needed to be settled, Miss Ashmore gave up thinking for the duration. She passed through the first day of Basil's absence like an automaton, saying and doing what she was supposed to, without really knowing or caring what it was.

The next day was much the same. She agreed to drive with Lord Arden and let him say whatever it was he had to say without contributing any brilliant insights of her own. *He* must have got a brilliant insight though, for they'd not been driving twenty minutes when he stopped the horses, preparatory to giving physical expression to what was on his mind.

This did rouse her from her trance. As she looked up into his face, now bent so close to hers, everything within her recoiled. She did not want him to touch her—not now, not yet. Another embrace was too fresh in her memory. She turned away, covered her face with her hands, and began to weep.

Now Miss Ashmore was not, in the normal way of

things, a watering pot, but philosophy had deserted her for the moment. Being miserable and not a little frantic, she found the tears came easily. She wept copiously, and nothing his alarmed lordship could say or do would calm her. Ten anguished minutes passed before she was finally persuaded to confide her trouble. By then, she'd made up her mind. Between hiccoughs, she told him what she'd learned, and what she suspected, and why she was afraid to confide the matter even to her godmother.

He looked puzzled at first, but in a very little while his face brightened into an abominably smug expression. "Why, you poor child. Is that all? You should have told me of this sooner. No wonder you've seemed so distracted the past few days."

Relieved to find that it was only a trifling matter of money that troubled her so, the marquess became transformed. He patted her hand in an indulgent, husbandly sort of way, dabbed lovingly at her tear-streaked face with his handkerchief, and went on to reassure her. It was the merest nothing, he told her. The Duke of Thorne's man of business would see about the details. They must think only of their future happiness.

While this was more or less what she'd hoped for, his personality change was not. Before he'd been the adoring suitor, striving to win her affection. Now he had conquered. To his mind, everything was settled. She was his. She'd confided in him—and hadn't she told him she'd confided in no one else? Wasn't he one of the few men in creation to whom a debt like Papa's was a mere trifle? The cocksure look on his face made her want to slap him. Still, there was something to be thankful for: he was too caught up in his triumph to remember to do more than squeeze her hand.

"Elope?" Alexandra repeated incredulously.

"Yes. It's the only way, don't you see?"

He'd drawn her and Jess out to walk in the shrubbery

the following afternoon. After summarily ordering his sister to make herself scarce, he'd come right to the point. Now, her insides churning, Alexandra stared stupidly at him. She hardly noticed that he'd taken both her hands in his, because that was only a minor detail of this nightmare. Telling herself she must wake up soon, she listened to him explain his Perfect Solution to their difficulties.

He'd decided that it was too risky to go about marrying in the normal, straightforward way. "An investigation will take time, and we can't risk it until after we're wed. Don't you see? I still can't go to your father and ask his consent, because he's obliged as a gentleman to refuse. As you said, it's a debt of honour to him. Moreover—if you'll excuse my saying so—he has struck me as being quite as obstinate as my own Respected Parent. If he denies me on the grounds of his obligation to Burnham, and I hint that Burnham is a bounder—well, what do *you* think will be the result?" He didn't wait to hear what she thought, only went on to reiterate that they must take matters into their own hands.

She'd brought it all on herself. If she'd let him speak to Papa in the proper way, in the first place, she might have had a great Society wedding, and crowds of people about. Now she must run away with him to Scotland, putting herself completely in his hands.

"B-but, my lord. You don't consider your family in this. To-to run off with the daughter of a mere baronet—and a penniless and eccentric one at that. They're bound to feel you've disgraced them—and they know nothing of me."

"Your father's family is an old and respected one. Your Mama was the grandniece of an earl. It's hardly as though I were running off with an opera dancer. Why do you torment me with these matters? Isn't it enough that I'm driven half-wild with fear that your father will any minute carry you away to Yorkshire? Do you realise that I dare not speak to him, for fear—*fear*, Alexandra—that it will drive him to do so?"

To expect the future Duke of Thorne to live in fear of

anything was to expect the planets to hurtle out of their courses in the heavens. To expect him to care anything what his relatives thought (if, that is, they had the effrontery to think differently than he did) was to expect the sun to rise in the west or Great Britain to sink into the sea. In short, it was futile to argue with him.

There being nothing to say, she was silent, listening and nodding her head while fervently wishing she had thrown herself over a ledge in Gjirokastra when she'd had the chance.

They'd elope the evening of Lady Dessing's birthday gala, three nights hence. Alexandra would not attend, because of one of her headaches. It was unlikely, he condescended to point out, they'd call in a physician for that; equally important, the household would leave her in peace.

As soon as the others left, she'd escape from the house, dressed in clothes he'd provide. With the servants belowstairs enjoying their leisure, she needn't fear detection. He'd slip away from the party to meet her, and they'd travel in disguise, using public conveyance for the first half of the journey. As to accommodations, as he tactfully put it, they'd travel as brother and sister.

Well, at least he didn't intend to deflower her before the wedding night. The technicality of marrying a virgin did, apparently, count with him—after all, the future Duke of Thorne was rather like a monarch, wasn't he? And like a monarch, he required from her only obedience. He would see to everything else.

= 14 =

EVERYTHING, TO HER regret, went as smoothly as Lord Arden had claimed it would, so that now—while the others were miles away, dancing at Lady Dessing's gala—Alexandra and the marquess were dining together in the Blue Swan coaching inn's only private parlour.

More strictly speaking, Alexandra was listlessly pushing her food around in circles on her plate. Interpreting her silence as prenuptial nerves, her considerate companion kept up an ongoing monologue between mouthfuls. The mail coach was due to arrive in an hour, he told her, and they had best fortify themselves. Given the eccentricities of public conveyance, the next few hours would be uncomfortable, but after that they'd travel in their own carriage. Though only a rented vehicle, it was, he assured her, comfortably sprung.

There was a light tap on the door, followed by the waiter. He was a surly fellow, with a great scarf wrapped about his head—for the toothache, he sulkily claimed—so that one could see little of his face but his nose. That was smudged with soot. He walked with a limp and with his head sunk to one side, as though he were in the habit of ducking, Alexandra thought with pity, the slings and arrows Life hurled at him. Will, having never been a victim of Life's cruel artillery, felt no such compassion. Majestically he gestured to the fellow to put the bottle down: "Mr. Fairstairs," as the marquess had chosen to style himself, would pour his own. Not that she could blame him. The waiter's hands were none too clean or too steady. Too bad, she reflected idly. Well-shaped and long-fingered, they might have been graceful hands, had Providence seen fit to give him the marquess's advantages.

Because Alexandra was greatly tempted to drink herself into insensibility, she confined herself to water. She took a sip, noted it was as bad as everything else, and forgot all about the waiter's existence.

Will hadn't forgotten, however. The door had hardly shut behind the fellow when Lord Arden wondered aloud what the landlord was thinking of to hire such a filthy, disgusting creature. He became very apologetic then about subjecting his Beloved to this shabby place. He said he hadn't expected it to be quite so bad, and he seemed to take it as a personal affront.

Well, of course. He was a Farrington, and the rest of God's creatures—with the possible exception of the Royal Family—were put on this earth for his comfort. Including herself. She'd come to suspect that the real reason he'd insisted on eloping was nothing more than the impatience of a spoiled, overgrown boy. What he wanted he wanted now, and without a lot of bother.

Not that he minded a little costume drama. The clerk's garb, for instance, that clashed ridiculously with his aristocratic mien. As she stopped glowering at her plate a moment to glance at him, Alexandra much doubted whether the landlord had been taken in. He'd "Yes, sir'd" and "If you please, sir'd" the marquess to death from the moment they'd stepped through the door. The whole business was absurd. They might have travelled in comfort in their own clothes. A few coins dropped here and there would have stilled eager tongues. But no, Will must make a whole production of it. It was obvious he thought it all most dashing and romantic.

Actually, it would have been romantic if he were someone else. If that were only another face across the table, and if those eyes had been amber instead of grey. If that voice droning on and on were a teasing mixture of ingenuousness and irony. But it was stupid to think of that, to think of *him*, when that only made her heart ache. She was wretched enough as it was. From the moment Will had proposed his scheme, it had never occurred to him to consult her wishes in anything. Not that she had any wishes any more—except that the coach would overturn along the way, and she be crushed to death beneath it.

Which was mere histrionic self-indulgence. After all, she wasn't running off with an ogre. He was handsome, wasn't he? And immensely rich and important. So what if he was spoiled and selfish. Weren't most of his peers? She was dutifully removing the scowl from her face and struggling to replace it with an affectionate smile when the marquess's voice mumbled off into silence. Looking up, she discovered to her amazement that Lord Arden's head had slumped to his shoulder and he was sinking in his chair.

Good grief! Was the man drunk? Yet he'd consumed only two glasses of wine with his meal, and he'd seemed cold sober when he'd come for her. Bewildered, she sat staring helplessly at her unconscious husband-to-be and frantically wracked her sluggish brains. What on earth should she do?

"What a stimulating dinner companion you've got to be, Alexandra. You've talked the poor man unconscious."

She sprang from her chair to turn towards the door, whence the voice had come, then only stood there, frozen. It was a nightmare. She'd been dreaming all this time.

"Or have you poisoned him at last, my love?" Basil asked as he sauntered over to have a look at the comatose marquess.

"What—what are you doing here?" she gasped.

"Rescuing you, my darling. As I always do. Dear me." His face assumed a theatrical expression of horror as he lifted Lord Arden's limp wrist then let it drop back onto the table. "I hope you haven't killed him. It'll be a job to keep you from swinging for it, lovely as you are, and sympathetic as the judge is sure to be when you tell him how Will had bored you past all endurance. But a peer of the realm, my dear. Or peer-to-be, actually. Shocking."

His wit, in this case, was entirely wasted. The young lady scarcely heard a word of it, being in the process, for the first time in her twenty-four years, of fainting dead away.

Though she was inexperienced in the business, Basil, fortunately, was not. He caught her up in his arms before she sank to the floor and carried her out of the shabby parlour.

"Just as I suspected," he told the innkeeper, who was hovering anxiously a little distance from the door. "It is my sister. There'll be a reward for you, my good sir. Your sharp eye has helped preserve an innocent female from disgrace. Now do you keep that eye on that villain there while I restore this poor, foolish child to her senses."

She felt something damp at her forehead, opened her eyes, then closed them again. Surely she was dreaming, had dreamt everything, and must be still lying in her comfortable bed at Hartleigh Hall. She could not be in this dingy room, and that could not be Basil sitting on the edge of the lumpy mattress, bending over her.

"Come now, Alexandra. Time to rejoin the living."

It *was* something damp—a towel—and it was Basil and not a dream. She opened her eyes again.

"That's better. What a turn you gave me. I never took you to be the swooning type. But then, I never knew you were another Lucrezia Borgia either."

"Good heavens!" She pulled herself up to a sitting position. "Surely he isn't dead—"

"No, he isn't, unfortunately. I gave him only enough medicine for a long sleep—not an eternal one. Though the temptation was strong enough," he added with a twisted little smile.

"You *drugged* him?"

"It was the best I could do on the spur of the moment.

Really, dear, I was never so shocked in my life—to see you enter this shabby place, dressed as—well, I could hardly tell what. The vicar's daughter, perhaps? Running off with her Papa's clerk? Was that it? Yet I'd never before heard a humble clerk order an innkeeper about in that imperious way. How fortunate for you I was here, my love. The story would have been all over the county in a matter of hours and sure to take all the shine out of Lady Dessing's birthday fête."

Shock was rapidly giving way to vexation. How could he chatter on so calmly—and Lord Arden lying somewhere unconscious. "What," she very nearly shrieked, "are you doing here?"

"Rescuing you, as I said."

"I didn't ask to be rescued."

"Didn't you? Yet I could have sworn when I saw you enter that you looked precisely as Marie Antoinette must have done when they led her to the guillotine."

"Never mind how I looked. Why are you here? You're supposed to be in London."

"Yes, I am. I'm such an unreliable fellow, you know. Never where I should be, doing what I should be." He still had the towel and was absently wrapping it around one hand, then disarranging it, then arranging it again as he spoke.

Dazedly she stared at the towel and at the hands playing with it. Light dawned. "It was you. *You* were the waiter," she cried accusingly.

"Yes, I was." His smile this time was so sweet and tender that her heart skipped a beat. "I couldn't, after all, trust Mine Host to so delicate a business, could I? Though he's most observant—calling my attention to the rum pair deigning to honour him with their patronage. I suspect he wants the subtle touch."

"But why? Why?" Even as she asked, she knew, or thought she knew, for one dizzying instant. But he looked away quickly, and she told herself she was overwrought and imagining things.

"Because the pair of you were about to spoil everything after I've been running myself ragged the past five days to make everything perfect." He tossed the towel onto a chair. "Now, though it complicates everything dreadfully, I'll have to take you both back. Did anyone see you on the road?"

"I don't know—but what are you saying? I can't go back now. Lord Arden and I—"

"Yes, my love. You were eloping, which is perfectly absurd."

"It isn't," she protested. "You don't know—"

"I know you're not going to Scotland with Will, as he can't go anywhere under his own power for the next several hours. I'm taking the two of you back. Now," he went on, consulting his pocket watch, "there are bound to be dilatory stragglers headed for Netherstone, so we'll have to keep off the main road. Fortunately, I know a shortcut—but then, so does half the world. Still, we can risk that if . . ." He nodded to himself. "Yes. That should do."

He got up from the bed and walked to a corner of the room, where he began rummaging in some bundles.

While he was thus engaged, she found her tongue again and set up a steady stream of objection, though, as he hadn't yet confided his plan, she wasn't sure what exactly she was objecting to. Nonetheless, she explained, albeit incoherently, about the increase in Papa's debt and how she'd had to confide in Will and how, if she didn't elope with the marquess, that left Randolph and his insufferable family. She might as well have saved her breath.

"Yes, dear," he patiently agreed. "I daresay it may be as you claim. If you'd only listened to me in the first place, you wouldn't be in such a predicament."

"L-listened to y-you?" she sputtered indignantly.

"Didn't I say I'd help you?"

"And then turned round and left for London," was the scornful rejoinder.

"Did you think I'd abandoned you, darling?" He approached the bed. In his hands was a pile of clothing which she barely looked at, being mesmerised by the sweet, fond look he bent upon her. Good grief—a few minutes alone with him and her mind turned completely to mush.

"I am not your darling," she snapped, rather savagely.

"As you like. Here." He dropped the garments into her lap. "Get into those."

She glared down at the little heap, and then blinked as she recognised what it was: his clothes. What on earth was he about? "Why?" she demanded. "Why must I go back?"

"Because I said so. Because you haven't any choice. Because anything you like, only do hurry up. We've got some hard riding ahead if you're to be back before the family is."

"I am not," she announced, folding her arms across her bosom in a very determined way, though, actually, it was to conceal its heaving, "going anywhere until I hear an explanation. It was bad enough having Will order me about all this time, when at least I knew why. But you appear out of nowhere and start dictating—"

"Darling, I'm only trying to help you," he said, soothingly, sitting down upon the bed again. "There isn't time to explain everything. Can't you just trust me this once?"

"*Trust* you?" Her voice dripped sarcasm. "You've only just drugged the future Duke of Thorne. Not to mention the fact that you've never behaved properly in all the time I've known you. Or done anything but tease and mock and lie. Trust you, indeed. I don't know why," she went on, angrily, "I ask you to explain, when you're bound to lie about that as well."

"I have, I agree, lied to everyone else on the whole blessed planet. But, Alexandra, to you I've hardly lied at all. Why do you scold so?"

He looked so genuinely baffled that she began to wonder

why herself. Oh, what was the use, anyhow? She dropped her gaze to her hands. "I'm tired," she said. "I'm tired and my head is spinning, and nothing makes sense. Now you tell me I must go back. Oh, Basil, how could you?"

"How could I what?"

"You left me," she blurted out. "You left me and let me think you were gone for good—" She stopped short, realising that she was on the brink of betraying herself.

"I'm sorry, my love. I shouldn't have." He took her hand in his. "But does it matter to you what I do?"

"No," she lied, snatching her hand away.

"No, of course it doesn't. It's too much to hope. No reason on earth you should trust me, is there?"

She shook her head.

"Not even when I'm only hours away from solving the Burnham problem once and for all?"

She looked up at him, suspicious still, though hope fluttered faintly within her.

"Not even," he continued softly, "if I say I do it all for you because it matters to me what becomes of you?"

She shook her head again automatically.

He went on more lightly, "No, I suppose there's no helping *that*—not now, at least. Well, then, here is the situation. We must get you and Will back for a hundred reasons I can't go into now. Except that I will have laboured in vain if you run off with him. I did understand—correct me if I'm wrong—you weren't really keen on doing so."

It was useless to pretend otherwise. "I wasn't," she admitted. "I'm not."

"Then won't you please do as I ask? I can give you about half an hour to change while I deal with the innkeeper and see about horses. I promise you, it means the end of the Burnham business—without alternative fiancés and husbands. I give you my word, my love."

Well, she hadn't any choice, had she, whatever his word was worth? Will was useless at present. And she could hardly go off by herself, even if she had anywhere to go. She acquiesced.

"Oh, you are wonderful." He dropped a light kiss on the top of her head, then left the room.

She stared at the door for a moment, her hand creeping up to touch the spot where his lips had been. Of everything that baffled her—how he came to be here, why he'd drugged Will, what this mysterious plan was to solve the Burnham problem—it was this that puzzled her most. All the usual endearments, the usual mix of melodrama and farce . . . then one small, affectionate gesture to upset all her conclusions.

It recalled that afternoon they'd ridden together, when he'd put aside his practised arts for a while and treated her like a friend. He'd promised to help her then. But if he'd meant it, why in heaven's name had he gone off without a word of explanation, letting her think he'd gone out of her life for good?

"Oh, Basil," she murmured to the empty room, "it's always 'why' with you."

The room making no suitable reply, she shook her head and turned to the business at hand.

It was a disconcerting and troublesome business. For one, there seemed to be at least nine thousand fastenings to unfasten before she could get out of her dress. For another, his clothes didn't fit. The shirt was too big, and his trousers, which were indecently snug about her hips, gaped even more indecently at the waist. Frenziedly, she unbuttoned the trouser flap and stuffed her shawl inside, as padding. It felt stupid, and looked stupider, but at least it helped disguise her unmasculine curves. Having no idea how to deal with the neckcloth and afraid to crumple it, she ignored it, and jerked on waistcoat and coat. Apparently, since he'd not supplied her with his footwear, her own half-boots would do.

It was the oddest feeling to be wearing his clothes. Though they were fresh and clean, something of him pervaded them—something that made her feel uncomfortably warm and flustered. Nervously she pulled and tucked and pushed at the garments. Then, when she was certain nothing more could be done to improve her appearance, she sat down on the edge of the bed and waited.

In a few minutes there was a light tap on the door and Basil's voice asking if she were decent.

"If you can call it that," she answered, turning pink. She turned pinker still when he entered the room and, after studying her for a moment, broke into a smile.

"You needn't laugh," she snapped. "You could hardly expect a perfect fit—and I hadn't a valet to help me."

"I would have been thrilled to death to valet you, my dear, if you'd only asked. Now, if you'll pin your hair up, I shall tie your cravat. In that at least you shall not be faulted."

She did as he asked. But when he stood so close to wrap the linen about her neck, her knees grew shaky and weak, and her heart promptly commenced knocking in concert.

He was, she thought, an unconscionably long time about it. When, finally, she began to express impatience, he retorted that it was no simple business when the cloth was about his own neck; to have to work *backwards* was a feat of inexpressible difficulty.

"And it doesn't help—" But he thought better of it and held his tongue.

No, it didn't help at all that Alexandra in trousers—in *his* trousers—was provocation beyond all endurance. His hands were unsteady. They wanted to be everywhere else but at this dratted piece of linen. Her padding only invited removal, and the ill-fitting coat . . . oh, that was even worse. To look at it was to imagine her wearing nothing but. Being cursed with a fertile imagination, he was plagued with more disconcerting visions still, with the result that he didn't dare move a muscle beyond those required to tie the cravat, for fear he'd lose all control, drag her to the bed, and ravish her.

Finally, the job he'd been a fool to undertake was done, and he could step away from her. "There," he said, turning away. "You'll do. Just put on your—my—hat, and let's get out of here."

With the innkeeper's assistance, Will was carried out and flung unceremoniously over Basil's mount. After a brief, whispered conversation and the clinking of coins, Basil leapt up behind the marquess's prostrate form.

"It's going to be deuced uncomfortable," he told his companion. "Both the horse and I had much rather it was you. But leading another beast would only slow us more. Ah, well." He gave a forlorn sigh, and they were on their way.

They reached Hartleigh Hall a little before midnight and rode quietly round to the servants' entrance.

"Now do you go on ahead," he whispered. "My valet was supposed to leave the door unlatched—"

"You've been here already?"

"No, but I sent Rogers. You must slip upstairs and go to my room. He'll be waiting. Tell him there's been a slight change in plans and that he's to come down to me."

"You want me to go to him looking like this?"

"My dear, Rogers cannot be shocked. It's out of the question. Besides, he's the most close-mouthed fellow in creation. And I must have his help in getting Will dressed and back to the party. Come." He strode over to help her down from her mount.

If he took the opportunity to hold her a little closer than was absolutely necessary for rather longer than was absolutely necessary, and if his lips touched hers before he let her go, it must be blamed on the excitement of the moment. As must, of course, Miss Ashmore's delay in letting go of *him*. In any case, there was a brief embrace, at the conclusion of which Mr. Trevelyan gave it as his opinion that she'd better go in quickly. She retorted that it was he who kept her back, which led to another, longer embrace and

Mr. Trevelyan's husky observation that if she didn't go in now he couldn't answer for the consequences.

"Then let go of me," she snapped with rather more ferocity than circumstances required, for he was not holding her so very tightly as all that, and she had suffered two kisses without giving any sort of battle.

At any rate, he did let go, and she fled, her face blazing with shame. She got upstairs undetected, found Rogers—who, as promised, never turned a hair at seeing her in his master's coat and trousers—and communicated her message. Then, red-faced again, she crept on to her own room, shut the door, and fell, shaking, onto the bed.

= 15 =

EMMY CLUCKED WITH sympathy as she placed on her mistress' lap the tray containing a steaming cup of coffee. "Oh, Miss, is it still bad then? You look as if you never slept a wink—and it's no wonder, such a to-do as we had last night."

Lifting the cup with two trembling hands, Alexandra informed her abigail that she'd never heard a thing, having slept like the very dead she was sure. That was true enough.

Basil had come to her door last night just as she was preparing to climb into bed. Yanking her dressing gown tightly about her, she'd gone to answer the knock. With no thought of decorum, he'd pushed the door open and strolled in as assuredly as though he'd dropped into his own club. He'd looked so elegant and handsome—every hair in place, his evening costume perfectly pressed and spotless—that she'd begun to think she'd imagined the whole evening's adventure.

It was only after his eyes raked her insufficiently clad form and he'd made a rather indecorous proposal that she'd collected her wits and seized the washbasin as a weapon. After declaring her cruel and heartless, he'd said he'd only come to take his clothes back and to tell her she must pretend she'd never left her room that night—no matter what Will might be foolish enough to say when he recovered.

Basil had gone on to explain that he must be away for a few days, but he begged her to trust him in the meantime.

"No one," he'd promised, "is going to drag you off to Yorkshire. So there's no need to fall in with any more of his lordship's schemes. Is that clear?" It wasn't clear, and she didn't like taking orders, but she'd nodded.

He'd then asked for a good-night kiss. Being threatened with the washbasin instead, he'd taken mournful leave of her, once more remarking on her want of feeling.

After he'd gone, she'd taken the laudanum her hostess had so thoughtfully provided earlier for her headache. It would have been impossible to sleep otherwise. She had, therefore, slept very soundly and never heard the others return. She did not mind that her tongue, at the moment, was thick and unpleasant-tasting in her mouth, or that her head felt as though it were in a vise. She'd had blessed oblivion for a few hours at least.

Emmy seemed about to burst with suppressed excitement.

"A to-do?" Alexandra asked, with admirable composure. "What sort of to-do?"

"Oh, Miss, every sort of thing. Mr. Burnham is gone off, no one knows where. His lordship—Lord Arden, that is—was carried up to his room, and I don't know what else. We were all at sixes and sevens and no one in their beds until sunup at least. That was only the ladies, as the gents was down in the library talking the longest time after."

As she took in her mistress's white, drawn face, Emmy was stricken with guilt, and began berating herself for upsetting the poor lady when it was plain she was still ill. She plumped up the pillows, straightened the coverlet, and left the room, still muttering at herself.

It was several hours before Alexandra heard the full story, as the rest of the family and guests remained in their beds until well into the afternoon. She dressed herself but, not caring to risk a confrontation with Lord Arden, kept to her room and tried to focus on Mr. Richardson's *Clarissa*. Though she'd read the old novel years ago in defiance of her governess, and though the interminable epistles did tax her patience dreadfully, Alexandra was determined to read the story through, "for the sentiment," as Dr. Johnson had recommended.

She would have preferred, certainly, that Lovelace did not so very much remind her of Mr. Trevelyan, and that Clarissa's parental difficulties did not make her own pale into insignificance. Nevertheless, she read on doggedly until Aunt Clem appeared to give her a full accounting of the night's events.

Lady Bertram told the tale in her usual blunt way. That rattle of a nephew of hers had put in a surprise appearance just as the party was going in to supper. He'd treated them all to some cockamamie tale about his horse stumbling into a ditch and the consequent several hours' delay which had prevented his arriving at Hartleigh Hall in time to accompany them to the gala.

Her ladyship communicated her private opinion that it was no four-footed creature that had delayed him but a barmaid, for he wore an insufferable cock-of-the-walk air that made his aunt want to slap him senseless.

At any rate, he'd exhausted himself during supper and a couple of sets after, cutting a swathe through all the debutante hearts in the vicinity. He'd gone out to the terrace for a breath of air. There he'd come upon Will who was sprawled out, unconscious, on one of the long stone benches.

"I'd wondered where he'd got to," her ladyship muttered. "Hadn't seen him for hours. Well, evidently he'd been fully occupied, drinking himself into stupefaction."

Lord Arden was bundled off to an unoccupied parlour while the festivities continued into the small hours of the morning. When it was time to depart, the servants carried him out to the carriage. Basil, who'd been supervising this procedure, was the one to find the note addressed to Sir Charles. It was lying on the seat of the vehicle in which the baronet had ridden to the gala.

At this point in the narrative, the countess's patrician

features broke into a grin of unholy glee. "What do you think, my dear? Your Papa's scholarly companion—the steadiest chap in the world, according to Charles—has run away. Run away!"

"Good heavens," said Alexandra, rather faintly.

It was true. Mr. Burnham had, according to his note, decided to take control of his own life for once. Though he'd worded it diplomatically enough, it was plain—to Aunt Clem at least—why he'd gone.

"Is it not astonishing, my dear? The dutiful boy blankly refuses to marry you."

"Yes, it is astonishing, Aunt Clem. Randolph Burnham running away. Randolph flouting his Papa's commands. I can scarcely credit it," said the young lady. Her face was pale, but her voice was steady enough.

"Well, credit it, my dear. Even your father, shocked as he was, was forced to believe his own eyes. I am sure that if he had not feared for Randolph's safety—for, in truth, as Basil said, the young man's an innocent lamb and might easily stumble into difficulties, left to himself—well, if that were not his main concern, he'd have shrugged it off soon enough. At any rate, Basil offered to go look for Mr. Burnham to reassure us all that the young man was safe. Obliging fellow, my nephew, isn't he?"

Miss Ashmore nodded.

"But I'll tell you, my dear, your father was not so very distressed by that note—though of course he grumbled and carried on. I was most pleased, as you can imagine. For you see what this means. Now, at last, you may have a proper Season."

Miss Ashmore must not have appeared as delighted at this prospect as the countess had expected, for her ladyship went on reassuringly, "Well, of course you must, Alexandra. Will's behaviour last night does make one wonder whether he's settled and mature enough to make an acceptable husband. I recognise, of course, that the gentlemen must indulge, but it is very bad form to show the extent of the indulgence. A man who cannot hold his liquor had better not drink it in the first place. Most especially not when he is endeavouring to win the esteem of a gently bred woman."

In the event the implications of this breach of etiquette had not already occurred to his lordship, his sister was in the process of bringing the matter forcibly—and at altogether unnecessary volume, he thought—to his attention. She stood over his bed of pain delivering a scathing lecture of nearly an hour's duration. This he was forced to endure in relative silence, having learned at the outset that no one knew anything of the aborted elopement. All assumed that Miss Ashmore had been sleeping innocently in her own bed the entire night.

When his sister—with the parting declaration that she fervently hoped Miss Ashmore would give him his *congé*— finally took herself off, Lord Arden considered the facts as he had them. It was not easy or pleasant to do so. His head felt as though his horse had been dancing upon it, and twice he had to abandon his meditations in order to retch into the chamber pot. Nonetheless, sick as he was, he saw plainly enough the fine hand of Basil Trevelyan in this business. Trev's sudden appearance so late at the gala. Trev finding him on the terrace.

Damn the intriguing, interfering devil! He'd arranged matters very neatly, very neatly indeed. The marquess could hardly accuse him openly without admitting his own guilty secret—and if he did, he must implicate Miss Ashmore. His hands were tied. After his allegedly low behaviour of last night, he must count himself lucky if allowed within fifty miles of the young lady. And, for the moment at least, there wasn't one blessed thing he could do about it.

"Basil?" Lord Hartleigh repeated, looking at his guest as though the fellow had just escaped from Bedlam.

He had, it was true, expected an apology. But the gothic accusations that followed made the earl wonder whether the young man should be sent back to bed and a physician called in. In the next few minutes, however, as Will summed up the suspicious circumstances, Lord Hartleigh was forced to admit to himself that this tale was very much in Basil's style.

"You know me, Hartleigh," the marquess pleaded. "When have you ever seen me make such a cake of myself? Why, if you called all Dessing's servants together and questioned them, you'd find I had no more than three glasses of champagne altogether."

"So you suspect Basil somehow slipped something into one of those glasses?"

Though Lord Arden meant other glasses at another place, he nodded grimly.

"Why? What had he to gain by it?"

"I'm not sure," the marquess hedged. "Though I can make a good guess, and I mean to set him straight."

"Well, that's only natural. Though I might add it's also a great waste of time. Basil can't be set straight. It's physically impossible. Besides, he's gone after Mr. Burnham."

"Yes, and I'm going after him."

"Now, Will, don't make a mountain out of a molehill. Whatever you suspect—"

"It's no secret that I have been endeavouring to win the affection of the young lady under your roof," Lord Arden interrupted rather pompously. "Last night's events are not calculated to inspire her confidence. I intend to clear this matter up—and with it my character."

In vain did the earl attempt to pour oil on the troubled waters. Will was determined to find Basil and wring the truth out of him. That failing, he would, he hinted darkly, seek other satisfaction.

Well, if he must, he must. Lord Hartleigh shrugged. Basil could take care of himself. Fortunately, not having the remotest idea where his cousin had gone, the earl was spared the disagreeable necessity of offering Lord Arden any other assistance than a reluctant "Godspeed."

My Lord Hartleigh, as was his habit in all things, confided the matter to his wife and was a little surprised to see her intelligent blue eyes lit with vexation.

"Gone after him?" she repeated. "And you let him, Edward? Gracious God! What if he kills him?"

"Of course he won't kill him. They've been playing pranks on each other and vowing revenge since they were boys. Will isn't about to risk disgrace and exile on account of a mere female—regardless how much he thinks he wants her."

"I still don't like it. This whole business has gotten completely out of hand."

"Which is what I predicted in the first place. There's nothing you or I can do now. Except, perhaps, report to your mother—as if she doesn't know already."

"Gone after him?" Lady Deverell repeated, bored past all expression. "How very wearisome in this heat." She returned her attention to the book that lay in her lap.

"Mama!"

"Yes, my love." The viscountess did not look up.

"What are we to do?"

"I suppose," Lady Deverell answered vaguely, apparently preoccupied with the book, "we shall have to dress soon. We are promised to the Osbornes for dinner. How distressing for them. With the three gentlemen gone, the numbers at table will be sadly out. How tiresome for Mrs. Osborne when she goes to so much trouble."

"She won't be tired at all if there's gossip to be gotten out of it," Isabella retorted. "I daresay it's all over the county by now after that scene at Netherstone. Mr. Burnham runs away, and then Basil goes after him for no apparent reason, and then Will after *him*. I wonder who'll be next?" She cast a speaking glance at her mother. In answer she received a world-weary shrug followed by a world-weary sigh. "I suppose," she told her provoking parent, "I had better let Miss Ashmore know of it."

"Why on earth should you do that, my love?"

"Because," was the exasperated reply, "she's bound to remark Will's absence sooner or later, and though you like to tease and make secrets of everything, I do not."

"Why, Bella, my darling, what on earth are you in such a pother about?"

"You, Mama. You know exactly what is going on and you tell me nothing, only sit there like the Sphinx. As though it were the most natural thing in the world that a quiet, studious gentleman like Mr. Burnham should take it into his head to run away. Or that Will Farrington, whose head for spirits is harder even than Papa's, would drink himself insensible. Or that Basil, who makes such a scene about going to London, should turn up at the Dessing's party five days later—and the party half over. Really, Mama, what a ninnyhammer you must think me."

Lady Deverell looked up from her book with a blank little smile. "Why, my dear, now you mention it, it is rather odd, is it not?" She shrugged philosophically. "Still, there's no accounting for the strange starts men will take. Don't trouble yourself about it, dear. Pray do not. I daresay there is a perfectly reasonable explanation for everything."

"Oh, I daresay there is," Isabella muttered, sarcastically. "Oh, indeed, there must be. But I'm not about to find it out from you, am I? No, of course not. Why should you condescend to tell your daughter anything?"

The viscountess only chuckled while Lady Hartleigh, feeling much inclined to shake her aggravating parent until her teeth rattled, told off the Fifth Commandment to herself and exited from the room.

Though she was in the company of her godmother when the news was told, Miss Ashmore could not keep her voice steady. "Gone after Mr. Trevelyan? But why on earth should he do that?"

"Will claims he wasn't foxed at all," Lady Hartleigh explained. "He insists that the little he did drink was adulterated with something else, and that it was Basil did the mixing."

Alexandra was very surprised to hear her godmother explode with laughter, as was Lady Hartleigh. The two stared at the older woman.

What on earth, Alexandra wondered, was so funny? Basil was in danger. He could be dead—even now—at Lord Arden's hands. It was horrible, and Aunt Clem was laughing!

"Now, now Alexandra. Don't take on so. Why, child, you look as if you'd seen a ghost. You too, Isabella. Why, of course it's nothing. They are always at each other, those two. Have been since they were children. Oh, but it is monstrous amusing." Lady Bertram wiped away the tears, chuckling as she did so.

"Yes," Isabella seconded, though with less assurance. "That is what Edward says. So you needn't worry about Will. He'll come to no harm, I'm sure."

It had not occurred to Miss Ashmore to worry about Will, but she didn't mind having this convenient excuse for her too-obvious agitation. She got through the rest of the conversation with as much poise as she could muster, which was little enough, though no one seemed to notice.

She managed to muster a bit more that evening when they dined with the Osbornes and some others, though the visit was ghastly. Those dreadful girls carried on so about the gentlemen's absence and dropped such thinly disguised hints about her devoted marquess's desertion that Alexandra wanted to throttle them. The Mama was even worse with a horrid smile pasted on her fat face as she asked two hundred times where all the young gentlemen had gone, and why and how.

The evening dragged on interminably. Between worrying about Basil, hating the Osbornes, and pretending all the while to be perfectly at her ease, Miss Ashmore was nearly dead with exhaustion when she climbed into the carriage to return to Hartleigh Hall.

Finally she could retreat to her bedroom, where the cumulative effects of not sleeping or eating properly and being consumed by anxiety resulted, quite logically, in hysteria.

The others were not unduly alarmed about either Basil or Will—but then, they didn't know what had actually happened last night. Though, when you came right down to it, neither did she. Obviously, Basil had had a hand in Randolph's disappearance; and given what he'd done to Will, Alexandra was afraid to imagine the criminal means employed in her other fiancé's case. She was afraid that even if Will didn't get to dispense his own justice, others would.

Basil lying cold and lifeless on the ground. Basil dangling from the end of a gibbet. Such visions were not conducive to rest. She lay awake, frightened and sick at heart and, yes, angry as well. It was bad enough to have fallen in love with a libertine. To be besotted with a villain—a criminal— well, that was the very acme and pitch of stupidity.

It cannot be expected that even one of so philosophical a turn as Miss Alexandra Ashmore could wait placidly for the denouement. She wept a great deal more than she liked when she was private, though she was able to behave rationally enough in company. She was used to pretending, after all. The past three months, it seemed, had been spent in one performance after another. It was only in the loneliness of her bedroom that she let herself give way. So it went: a performance by day and misery by night, as the days and nights passed and there was no word.

= 16 =

"Mr. Latham, I will not have it!" Mrs. Pamela Latham pushed the startled housemaid back into the hall, shut the door, and advanced upon her husband.

"Have what, my dear?" the gentleman asked mildly, removing his spectacles.

"That horrid creature is back again, and I'm sick of the sight of him. Wherever he goes trouble follows." Mrs. Latham collapsed into a chair, her ample bosom heaving. "Was it not he who came with that wicked man in the first place? Was it not he, back again just a few days ago? Now Marianne is *ruined*. Ruined! And the beast dares to show his face again, smiling and preening himself like a sneaky tomcat."

Her husband, who'd been thoughtfully polishing his spectacles during this tirade, now put them back on again. "But my dear, he's not the tomcat who made off with your daughter. So hadn't you better have him shown in?"

There were ominous signs that his calm assessment of the situation would drive his wife into one of her hysterical fits. Happily, he was able to forestall this dangerous prospect by means of quiet but firm words. In another five minutes, Mrs. Latham was herself again. She haughtily bade Mary show the gentleman in to Mr. Latham's study and then see speedily about some refreshment.

"Well then, Basil, it is just as we thought." Mr. Latham spread out a pile of papers before his guest.

"Actually, it's as Randolph thought. He was certain that Sir Charles's travel accounts had been well received though in a quiet way. My own experience with them showed that the baronet is a frugal traveller. Yes, his so-called patron had ample return on his small investment."

"Well, your aunt suspected as much, you know."

There was a brief silence—hardly more than a few seconds—before Basil answered, easily enough, "Did she now?"

"Or did I neglect to mention that she'd written to me after George returned her bank draft? Yes, it troubled me from the first," he went on, running his eyes over the sheet he held in his hand. "Until you got Randolph talking, I was stymied. George keeps his affairs mighty close. Fortunately, Randolph made a few accurate guesses about his father's business associates, and once I tracked them down it was a simple matter. Their records did not match with what George reported to Ashmore. He'd kept two sets of ledgers, you see. Such a pity, when Ashmore never bothered to examine the accounts."

"Our irascible baronet cares only about the work itself, difficult as that is to believe. He wants a better keeper, Henry." Basil lounged back in his chair and smiled. "At any rate, between Randolph's defection and our evidence, I doubt Mr. George Burnham will care to give any more trouble."

"If he thought to, I expect he'll think again when he gets my letter. Marianne and Randolph will be enjoying their honeymoon by then, no doubt."

"Oh, yes. They had less than two full days' journey to Gretna Green."

"Good." Mr. Latham nodded with satisfaction. "My wife is still a tad overset. She wanted titles for all the girls, you know. Wants them all to do the same as Alicia."

"Still, she has two more unwed daughters."

"If they make matches one half as satisfactory as their older sisters', I shall count myself the most fortunate of

Papas. Randolph is a good, honest man, and we must make shift to tolerate his family's frailties. If Marianne is content, that's all that counts." The genial businessman looked over his spectacles at his companion. "And what of you, sir? All this hard work and trouble—and no reward in it for you? Perhaps you'd have done better to have stayed in India or Greece. Certainly there'd have been more profit in it, eh?"

Mr. Trevelyan's smile faded. "I wish to heaven I'd never gone to Greece," he muttered, half to himself. Noting his friend's uplifted eyebrow, he went on quickly, "But then, I'd never have stumbled upon this Burnham business, and Randolph would never have come here—"

"—and fallen in love with my daughter. Well, how fortunate you did stumble upon this Burnham business, as you put it. Come," the older man said briskly, "let us give you a proper meal. May we offer you a bed this night?"

Basil accepted the offer of sustenance but declared his determination to go back to Hartleigh Hall. "I can get there sooner than a letter can and will enjoy breaking the news myself."

"The news. Ah, yes, so you will. So you will."

"But first, Henry, I believe there is some information you wish to share with me."

Mr. Latham looked over his spectacles at his guest. "Is there, sir?"

"My aunt, Henry. What exactly has my aunt to do with all this?"

For all that he hadn't had more than one night's sleep in three, and for all his eagerness to be back at Hartleigh Hall, Basil did have some consideration for his beast. He stopped several times to rest his horse. Hunger had finally caught up with him, if weariness had not, when he reached the Dancing Pig.

While the hostler saw about his mount, Basil made his way into the tiny inn and ordered a little light refreshment from his hostess, the plump owner of the place.

He was just swallowing his last morsels of bread and cheese when the door to the snuggery opened and Lord Arden burst in.

"You—you bastard!" the marquess shouted, as he launched himself upon his startled victim. His attack was so unexpected and immediate that Basil had no time to react. As Will's fingers closed around his throat, Basil tumbled backwards helplessly in his chair onto the floor.

It was not the first time, however, that an irate gentleman had attempted to throttle him. Basil's survival instincts quickly taking over, his knee shot up. In an instant Lord Arden had rolled off him onto the floor and was curled up in a fetal position, gasping in agony as he clutched at certain parts of his aristocratic anatomy.

"Good heavens, Will," Basil told the writhing form of his childhood playmate. "What a turn you gave me." He picked himself up, dusted himself off, and straightened his cravat. He'd just restored the chair to an upright position when the hostler came stomping through the door with the hostess behind him, brandishing a broom.

"Here now," the man growled. "We won't have any brawling here. This is a respectable place."

"Why so it is," Mr. Trevelyan calmly agreed. "And as you can see, there's no brawl. Only that his lordship has been suddenly taken ill."

His lordship groaned.

"Now," Basil continued, "if you'd be so kind as to bring in a bottle of your best brandy, perhaps we can help restore the gentleman to rights."

The phrase "his lordship" had a magical effect, and the coins Mr. Trevelyan dropped into a plump, feminine hand an even more miraculous one. The two respectable persons took themselves off, bowing and curtseying as they went. A few moments later, the required bottle of brandy was carried in by the beaming hostess.

"Now, Will," said Basil, as he helped his companion to his feet. "Come sit down and have a glass with me. Tell me what on earth you were thinking of to pounce on me in that savage way."

If the marquess thought of pouncing again, the sight of the golden beverage being poured into a glass must have distracted him, for he did sit down dazedly and take the drink offered him.

It was not the first time he and Basil had scuffled, nor was it the first time that hostilities had been followed up by olive branches in liquid form. At any rate, he knew—and if he didn't, Basil was prompt to call it to his attention—that murder had a rather unwholesome effect upon one's reputation. The murder, moreover, of one of the ton could very easily lead to more unwholesome effects upon one's health. A noose, for instance, was prodigious unhealthy.

Still, the provocation had been very great. "What in blazes did you mean by interfering in the business, Trev? We were on our way to Gretna Green."

"I was only trying to help you, Will."

The marquess shook his head in dazed incredulity. "Help me?"

"Yes. Good heavens, man. How could I stand idly by, knowing the sort of fate that awaited you?"

Lord Arden had any number of "hows" in reply, as well as the very cold assertion that he hadn't asked for any help. But Basil bade him drink and be calm, and the marquess wanted the drink badly. His head throbbed, and he was exhausted after four days spent scouring the countryside. Also, at the moment, certain more vital areas of his anatomy were throbbing as well. He gave a resigned sigh and brought his glass to his lips.

"I myself," Basil informed him, with a pitying look, "have not once, but several times, nearly tripped the parson's mousetrap on her account."

"Oh, come, Trev. Tell me another one."

"It's the truth. Why, she very nearly had me in Albania. Why do you think I kept away from my aunt's house after my return? The fact is, upon discovering that I couldn't keep my hands off your prospective bride if she was within reaching distance, I was obliged to keep myself out of reach."

Basil went on to assert that he would have stayed away had he not been alarmed on his friend's account. He knew he couldn't warn his friend as it was bound to be taken ill. Still, Basil had felt obliged to come and keep an eye on things.

"Oh, really, Trev. You expect me to believe that was all out of concern for me?"

"Well, perhaps not entirely. Knowing you're a wise fellow, on to every trick, I was naturally curious how long it would take you to understand precisely what you were up against." To forestall any hasty defences of Miss Ashmore's honour—and Will was showing signs of rather homicidal hastiness—Basil refilled his companion's glass.

"I'm not trying to slander your Intended," he placated. "But think, Will, for once. Just think what a merry dance she's led you already. Think, too, of the hundreds of Eligibles your Mama has paraded before you, and ask yourself which one of them could have kept you so long a-wooing and driven you to such desperation. Ask yourself how it came to be that you, the future Duke of Thorne, must drag your intended bride off to Scotland in the dead of night in order to be sure of her. And ask yourself, while you're at it, just how sure of her you'd ever be. Ask yourself what pleasure you could take in your mistresses with your mind always on your wife, wondering what she was up to—and with whom."

Lord Arden asked himself these questions and must have found the answers unnerving, for his hand shook a little as he carried the glass to his mouth. He took a very long swallow while he studied his companion's face.

"You don't mean to say, Trev, that you think she'd play me false?"

"I mean to say," was the composed reply, "that the British male population would give you reason to worry.

Which, I daresay, is nearly worse. How could you leave her out of your sight knowing there were hundreds like myself, quite unable to keep their hands off her? Of course, you could leave her in the country—but even the country is not so secure a place for unattended wives, as any number of unhappy husbands might tell you. You see the problem, of course. If she could put even *you* into a fever to be shackled, then what effect do you think she'll have on lesser men? The fact is, Will, the woman's a menace to the national peace. Do you know what they called her in Albania? The English Witch. Because even the Albanian men—who think women a species of cattle—were obsessed with her."

As Basil went on to describe the extremities to which Dhimitri had been driven, Lord Arden found himself, for perhaps the first time in his self-indulgent life, thinking twice about something he'd set his mind on having. It confused him. He wanted Alexandra Ashmore as his wife mainly because it was unthinkable that so splendid a creature should grace any other home, carry any other name, bear any other children than his. However, it was also unthinkable that the future Duke of Thorne must submit to the indignity of living in his wife's pocket for fear of being cuckolded. What time would he have for women and gaming and drinking and all the other pleasures his vast wealth practically demanded if he must be forever fending off jackals like Trev?

Like Trev. Will's eyes narrowed. "You want her for yourself, Trev. That's why you warn me off."

"Of course I want her for myself," was the amiable reply. "Didn't I just say so? And I promise you, Will, if you marry her I'll be there in my hunting pinks with the rest, after your lovely fox. I tell you, I can't wait for her to be wed, because until she is I must keep to the sidelines. As you told me once, Auntie is standing guard. One false move and *I'd* be the nervous, horn-sprouting husband. Though I'm not nearly as possessive as you are and needn't worry about the family honour—after all, that's Edward's lookout, isn't it—still, it's bound to be an irritating sort of existence, don't you think? All those duels, for one thing. So tiresome."

The poison was taking its effect along with the brandy. In another couple of hours, as Basil went on to paint increasingly grim pictures of what the future held for any man rash enough to marry Miss Ashmore, Lord Arden was brought to heel.

He was, in fact, sick of the whole business. True, she was a priceless ornament to add to the Farrington possessions. But she was also, he was forced to admit to himself, incomprehensibly unresponsive to him. It would be pleasant to get back to his far less taxing twins in London. Relieved to have a face-saving excuse for abandoning the tiresome chase and more than a little foxed, he confessed aloud that Lust had blinded him to Consequences, went on to recite some sentimental poetry, and was soon admitting maudlinly that Basil was the very best of fellows, the very best indeed. A man couldn't ask for a better friend and couldn't deserve him if he did.

If Mr. Trevelyan had a conscience, it must have been moved by these expressions of brotherly feeling; but as he hadn't, it wasn't. Besides, he'd done no more than tell the truth, only tinted and arranged it to suit his purposes. After all, Basil silently replied to the thing muttering at the back of his mind that was not a conscience, it could all turn out as he'd predicted. Alexandra didn't love Will, and Will didn't really love her. If he did, he'd have been willing to risk all—the devil with his future peace of mind, his mistresses, and all his other trivial occupations.

Having in this wise quieted the troubling inner voice and having divided the remnants of the brandy bottle, Basil proposed a final toast, "to friendship." Thereafter he suggested that they find themselves beds for the night.

"A bed. Yes," his lordship agreed thickly. "Another lonely bed. Nearly a month of it, Trev. Though that's over, eh?" But as he was rather inelegantly rising from his chair, a thought struck him forcibly enough to make him fall back into it again. "Trev, it isn't over. The girl . . . I proposed. Half a dozen times at least."

"There were no witnesses."

"No." The marquess shook his head and blinked several times, trying to focus and looking amazingly like Freddie. "But still. Honour. Obliged, you know." He stared owlishly at Basil.

"Not at all. You disgraced yourself. Remember? Thanks to me. And though Miss Ashmore knows the truth, she can hardly admit it. With this cloud over you, no one would expect you to have the audacity to offer for her. Nor would my formidable aunt allow her to accept you if you did. No, don't worry about it, Will. Now let us go get some rest."

$=17=$

LORD HARTLEIGH'S FAMILY and friends were gathered in the sunny breakfast room, peacefully attending to their morning meal, when Basil and Will came sauntering in just as cavalier and careless as you please.

It took all of Alexandra's self-control, amid the ensuing pandemonium of questions and exclamations, to keep from leaping out of her chair and throwing her arms around Basil's neck. Though by now her body should have used up its supply of saltwater, tears of relief filled her eyes, and his face swam before her . . . for a moment. Then it wanted only another moment before the tears dried up of their own accord.

He never even looked at her. True, the others were raising a terrific clamour, and he was kept busy making clever retorts. Still, he might spare her a glance instead of dropping so coolly into the chair next to Jess—at the other end of the table. Will, the faithless fribble, couldn't spare his Intended a glance either. He only stood by the door, smiling appreciatively at the witticisms of his erstwhile rival. Gone after Basil, indeed. To carouse with him no doubt. To share some unspeakable dissipation or other. As disagreeable visions of buxom barmaids and chambermaids paraded through her head, her feminine flutterings of concern and relief precipitously gave way to rather unfeminine heavings of fury. Oh, she wished they *had* killed each other, the selfish beasts.

Miss Ashmore was so busy working herself into a rage

that she barely heard the conversation. It was not until she heard the gasps of surprise and Jess's "Oh, Lud!" that Alexandra called herself to attention.

"Eloped!" Lady Hartleigh exclaimed.

Alexandra's head jerked up, and her whole body began to tremble. But no one was looking at her or Will. They were all fixed on Basil, who answered with a little smile, "That's what I said. Randolph has run away with Miss Marianne Latham to Gretna Green. Actually, they're not running any more. By now they must be wed."

Lord Tuttlehope blinked uncomprehendingly at his wife, who blinked back.

"Marianne?" Alicia gasped. "Run away with Marianne?"

"Why, yes," said Basil. "Why do you think she was so obsessed with Athens and Sparta? You yourself remarked it. Not once but many times have I heard you complaining about those tiresome Penelope Wars. You see, when Mr. Burnham and Sir Charles visited, the two young people took a liking to each other. That much even I dimly noticed. I did not, however, imagine it was as serious as it turned out to be."

"But if it was so serious, why elope?" Jess asked.

"One assumes that they believed their respective families would object. Mrs. Latham, you see, wanted Marianne to have a London comeout with Alicia as chaperone."

"Oh, dear," said Alicia in sudden comprehension. "Mama and her titles."

"So, obviously, she wouldn't look kindly upon a wool merchant's son. Moreover, it appears that Randolph's parents also had other plans for him." This was communicated with nary a glance at Sir Charles, who sat speechless, gazing at Basil as though he were Lord Elgin's caryatid suddenly come to life.

Miss Ashmore stared at her plate.

"At any rate," Basil continued, "our two young lovers must have decided it was futile to attempt to bring their respective parents around. Randolph leaves Westford in despair. Then letters are secretly exchanged. The plot is hatched . . . and the two took the only course open to them."

At this point, several at table recollected Randolph's misery upon his arrival and how his spirits had miraculously undergone improvement.

"I thought it was because he'd taken a fancy to Hetty," Alicia admitted ruefully. "They were so cheerful together at that picnic."

While the others carried on noisily about this startling news, Miss Ashmore occupied herself with the story between the lines. No wonder Basil had been so friendly with Randolph. Having wormed his way into the young scholar's confidence, thereby learning of the hapless romance, Basil must have persuaded Randolph to elope. Certainly it wasn't the sort of notion Randolph would conceive on his own.

Now all made sense. The Blue Swan—the nearest mail coach stop on the road north—the night of the gala when, in the great crush of people, the disappearance of a guest or two was less likely to be remarked. And Basil, helpful as always, at the inn to see that everything went according to plan. Randolph had only to board the coach, meet Marianne, and travel on with her to Scotland. Yes, Basil must even have arranged how the young woman was to meet her lover without arousing suspicion. No wonder he'd been so adamant about getting the other elopers back to Hartleigh Hall. Only one wedding was required to scotch George Burnham's scheme.

She stared unseeing at the eggs congealing on her plate. For her, he'd said. He'd done it all for her. He could have let her go off with Will if he didn't care . . . but no. Her disappearance would cause more of an uproar than Randolph's. She and Will might easily have been caught and stopped, for Will's disguises had only made them more conspicuous. She, Will, Randolph, and Marianne, all on the same coach. Good heavens, what a farce. Everything would have been ruined, just as Basil had said.

Yet he could have told her. He could have taken her into his confidence instead of leaving her to make herself miserable over him for five whole days.

Fortunately for her fraying temper, the group broke up at last. While the others were filing out of the room, Basil took Sir Charles aside. "Mr. Latham asked me to put this into your hands," Mr. Trevelyan explained *sotto voce* as he slipped the baronet a letter. "You'll want to read it in private, I daresay."

Alexandra, who'd been hovering nearby, overheard the exchange and saw the envelope. Consumed with curiosity, she followed her father to the library. He sat down at the small study table where Mr. Hobhouse's *Travels in Albania* lay open awaiting his perusal. She sat down across from him and watched as he unfolded the paper and read, apparently oblivious to her presence.

When he got to the end, he gave a faint whistle in surprise and then began at the beginning again. This made Alexandra very impatient indeed. When he'd finished for the second time, she burst out, "For heaven's sake, Papa, what is it? What does it say?"

As the baronet returned from someplace apparently far away, she saw the familiar furrows settling into his forehead. "What does it say? What does it say? Only that I've been played for a fool these ten years and more. George Burnham has been cheating me. *Cheating* me, Alexandra. I can scarcely credit it. Yet the evidence is there, Mr. Latham says. He's talked to those with whom George dealt and seen their records for himself."

His daughter snatched the letter from his hands and read it. "Good grief!" she exclaimed softly. When she was done, she dropped the letter onto the table and looked at her father. Her eyes were filled with compassion—though what beat in her breast was great relief. "Oh, Papa. How disappointing for you. You trusted him—with everything."

"The more fool I," her father muttered. "Who'd have thought there could be so much deceit in this world?"

Her conscience pricked her. "Why you know there is, Papa, as there has always been, because men are greedy for money and power. Without greed, very likely there would have been no Peloponnesian War. No wars at all, probably. No civilisations toppled and rebuilt. All history an open book. No mysteries. Then think how bored you'd be."

He mustered up a wan smile. He was not, after all, entirely without a sense of humour, though it had been cruelly tried in recent months. "Still, it is not pleasant to contemplate how I've been taken in," he growled.

The accusing look he bent upon Alexandra made her a tad uncomfortable. Hastily she replied, "You must look on the bright side. I know you think highly of Mr. Latham. Didn't you once tell me you wished it was he had the care of your troublesome finances? And doesn't he say in his letter that he took the liberty of looking into these matters in the hopes of discovering some means by which he might act as your partner in future? Does he not offer to do so now in the kindest and most gentlemanly way? And his reputation is of the highest. Why, half the peerage has dealings with him."

It took some time. The baronet persisted in grumbling about deceit and trickery. Mr. Trevelyan's name was mentioned more than once with doubt and suspicion. Alexandra's own lack of forthrightness was remarked upon, but at length Sir Charles grumbled himself into a state of weary resignation. Consequently, when she mentioned Lady Bertram's wish to take her to London for the Little Season and the generous offer to take charge of her until a suitable husband was found, the baronet offered no objection.

He would be glad, he told his daughter bluntly, to have her off his hands now that he was free of his obligations. Yes, she might go with Clementina for as long as she liked. He was tired of keeping track of her suitors and fiancés. He wanted to go back to Albania where a man might do his work in peace. Dead civilisations and the dead who'd belonged to them were not nearly so troublesome as one unmanageable daughter aided and abetted by an interfering, overbearing old woman and her unspeakable nephew.

Alexandra listened patiently to his complaints, and when he was bored with them at last she took herself away. Putting aside Henry Latham's letter, he turned to Mr. Hobhouse's work, and in a very little while the furrows erased themselves from his brow.

"Eloped, did they?" Lady Jess said to her brother. She'd followed him to the billiard room where she was in the unladylike process of soundly trouncing him. "Just like that. And I suppose Basil never had a hand in it."

"If he had, he hasn't confided it to me."

"Hasn't he? And you two suddenly the best of friends." One more stroke was sufficient to dispatch her brother. She stood back, surveying the domain of her triumph while absently rubbing the tip of her billiard cue against her temple, smudging it with chalk. "What happened, Will? One minute you can't bear to have her out of your sight for an instant. Today you can't get far enough away from her. What happened when you met up with him?"

Lord Arden only shrugged and put his own cue away.

"You've given up, haven't you?" she persisted.

"You know, Jess," he said, taking her cue from her and putting it away as well, "you really oughtn't to play billiards at all. But if you must, you certainly should not win against a gentleman."

"Then there's no problem beating *you*, is there? Come, tell me. Have you given up or what?"

Her brother gazed down disapprovingly at her. Really, such a hoyden she was. All of twenty-three, and still unmarried. Well, that wasn't surprising was it? What chap wanted a wife who acted like another chap?

"I have decided," he said coldly, "that we shouldn't suit."

"Oh, you have, have you? Well, who do you think will suit you, you inestimable treasure? One of your ballet

176

dancers? Or perhaps one isn't enough. Perhaps you want a matching pair like those redheaded sisters—"

"Your mouth wants washing out with soap, sister dear."

"Will all great Neptune's ocean wash *you* clean of your sins? Come now, Will. After you'd got all my hopes up, you might as well tell me why I'm to be disappointed. Besides, I've beat you fair and square, and you owe me a forfeit."

The marquess bent a withering look upon his sister which she met with perfect equanimity, being immune to the devastating force of his personality. Knowing that she'd plague him until she was satisfied and fully aware that fabrications would be a waste of breath, he gave in and told her. Not everything, but enough to make her understand. When he was done, she gave a little whistle of surprise that made him wince. Plague take her! When would she ever learn to behave like a lady?

"Egad, Will," she cried. "You gave up because you thought she was too much for you to handle?"

"I thought the effort required was excessive," he replied dampeningly. "I don't want a wife who requires so much managing."

"Or one who might manage *you* is more like it. Lud, you're a greater fool even than I thought, to give up such a jewel for so paltry a reason. But it's just as well, I suppose. It's obvious you never intended to mend your ways on her account, and that would leave me to comfort her while you were out leaping from one poxy bed to the next. Well then, I suppose I should be thankful Basil opened up your eyes, if he spared me that unpleasant duty. Obliging of him, wasn't it?"

Her brother made no reply. He found his sister exceedingly tiresome today. He gave her one last cold, haughty stare and exited from the room.

"Yes, very obliging," Jess muttered to herself as she played absently with a billiard ball. "And what, I wonder, makes him such a philanthropist all of a sudden? Wretched, interfering beast."

"Egad, Maria," said Harry Deverell, as he strolled with his wife along the very same sheltered path two couples had trod several days before. "You haven't any scruples, have you? Half the servants spying for you, the other half spying for Clementina—and then to wring family secrets from Jess after using her brother so unconscionably. Really, my lady."

"But my love, when I saw her out in the garden stomping back and forth in such a temper, I was so afraid she'd catch her gown against the rose bushes and shred it to pieces. I only asked her if she was feeling poorly from the heat when immediately she launched into a perfectly exhausting catalog of her brother's flaws of character. Then, quite on her own—for really, I never prodded her in the least—she told me what Will had told her."

"So Basil frightened him off, did he? Well, I must say your confidence in the wretch proves to have been very well placed. Randolph, Will, even the great debt—all dispatched in less than a week. Amazingly efficient, isn't he, once he sets his mind to something? No wonder Henry Latham speaks so highly of him."

"Yes, dear. But it's the setting his mind in the first place that's so fatiguing. So obstinate, you know."

"Ah, well. He's used to doing just as he pleases. When you think what a way he has with the ladies—why, they're mere clay in his hands—it's no surprise he can't bring himself to settle on one."

Lady Deverell sighed in sorrowful agreement. "Ah, yes. You charming wretches. It is such great sport for you to play fast and loose with our tender feminine hearts."

"Yes, madam. Great sport indeed. Speaking of which, is this the romantic site you told me of? The scene of stolen interludes, jealous hearts, tears, and I don't know what else?"

They had, in fact, reached the site of recent highly charged events—the place, in short, where Lord Arden had attempted to compromise his Intended. Lord Deverell, having been obliquely accused of certain sporting instincts and furthermore seeing that the place was altogether satisfactory in every respect, determined to live up to the accusation and swept his wife into his arms. That vulnerable creature being, as she'd hinted, no proof against such wicked masculine wiles, gave herself with a low chuckle over to the conqueror.

═ 18 ═

IF ANYONE DESERVED a good night's sleep, it was himself. Yet Mr. Trevelyan was strangely reluctant to take himself to bed. He took another turn in the garden, and then another, but the cool fragrance of the country night did not soothe him. It had, after an hour's aimless pacing, only brought back vividly another garden far away and another night many weeks ago . . . and a pair of startled green eyes, searching his face.

He'd felt those eyes reproachfully upon him today and had been quite unable to meet them. He should have told her. It had been unkind—at the least—to leave her in the dark. But to see her arrive at that inn on Will's arm . . . well, in a matter of minutes, Basil had gone from jealous rage to guilt and back again. Yet, he'd been very high-handed with her—the more so because he knew he was to blame. Had he confided in her before he left, she could easily have found a way to put Will off.

But no. He'd been all in a dither then, too—because she'd proved, once and for all, how helplessly besotted he was, and because she'd laughed at him just when he was on the brink of confessing it.

He turned and made his way back to the house. Another long, lonely night then. Only this time he'd better think, and to the point. He'd have to speak to her tomorrow. "And say what, you great ass?" queried a mocking voice in the back of his head. "What do you think she'll believe *now?*"

Alexandra sat up and pounded her pillow, though her anger was hardly the pillow's fault. It was, however, an inanimate object upon which she might vent her frustrations with impunity—though it would have been ever so much more satisfactory to be pounding upon Mr. Trevelyan's head and tearing out his tawny hair by the clumpfuls.

For the tenth or twentieth time since she'd retired for the night, she flung herself back down upon the bed and closed her eyes. And for the tenth or twentieth time she cursed the day she'd met him.

The fact was that, like a great many other people whose prayers the gods have answered, Miss Ashmore was wishing she'd worded her orisons more carefully. True, being in love with the man, she must be overjoyed that he'd returned safe and sound. The problem was that, in returning not only unscathed but unchanged and therefore unimproved, he made her feel like an idiot. Virtually everything she'd thought and done from the minute she'd met him had been wrong. She'd driven herself distracted, trying to manipulate her father and Will by turns and had succeeded only in twisting herself deeper into a quagmire. From which Basil had, with hardly a second's thought, extricated her. A snap of his fingers and Randolph, Papa, George Burnham, and Will were all disposed of simultaneously.

There she'd been, plotting and worrying by day, worrying and weeping by night—a prodigious waste of energy. She was a fool. Her brains must have rotted away in the sultry Mediterranean climate.

Look at her prowling about the house and grounds all day today by herself, hoping like a sentimental goose that he'd come to her. Then what? Fall to his knees declaring that he did it all because he loved her? And in some treacly way straight out of a fairy tale, swear always to be faithful because now he'd found his one, his only, his *true* love at last.

Faithful, indeed. It was all a game to him, to play with others' lives. Hadn't Aunt Clem said it? It was a matter of pride with him to succeed completely in whatever he undertook, "particularly if it is something devious." All of this meant no more to him than what he'd done when he was abroad. Why confide in her? Why bother even to talk to her? She was only another of his pawns. Now he'd tied up all the loose ends he'd be gone again. Back to London and his usual dissipations.

If only he could go out of her life as well. But she was going to London herself in another two days, where she'd have to endure a Little Season, catching glimpses of him now and then at some party or other, watching him dance and flirt and reduce other ladies to inbecility. Doubtless she'd hear as well of much worse, for the gossips of London were indefatigable. No matter was too small for their prying eyes and malicious tongues.

That sort of thing she didn't need to witness or be told of. She was already jealous of the hundreds of young women she imagined in his arms because, fool that she was, she wanted him all to herself. How she'd missed him! But when she felt the tears starting in her eyes, she quickly took herself in hand. She would not weep another instant over him.

The clock in the hall struck one. Good grief! Nearly two hours she'd lain here making herself mad. Enough. If she couldn't sleep, at least she could read. There was always the interminable *Clarissa*, and she had finally got to the last volume. As she was getting up, about to light the candle on her bedstand, she remembered that she'd left the book downstairs in the library last evening. Well, no help for it then. She must either go down and get it or stay here and madden herself all night.

She crawled out of bed, pulled on her dressing gown, stubbed her toe on a footstool, and stumbled against the bedpost, but eventually got out of the room. Quietly and very cautiously—not wanting any more bruises—she made her way downstairs and groped along the hall. Having narrowly missed collision with the heavy table that stood by the library door, she found the door handle and opened the door.

Light. There was light in the room, and it was occupied. A single candle burned in a silver holder upon an elegant mahogany table. The soft candlelight bathed the room in a dreamlike, golden glow, and lounging at his ease on the great leather sofa was Mr. Trevelyan.

He was fully dressed except for his coat, which was draped over a nearby chair. His neckcloth dangled carelessly, and his tawny hair, glinting gold like new-minted coins under the soft light, was tousled—the result, no doubt, of being raked with his fingers. Even now he ran his hand through it as though bedevilled by something.

He looked up from the letter he'd been reading and stared at her for a moment as though disbelieving the evidence of his own eyes. Then a slow smile lit his handsome face.

Really, it was most unfair, she thought crossly. He had no right to be so beautiful, draped upon the sofa like some sly Apollo come down among mortal women to destroy their peace. It was positively cruel what that smile did to her. It made her want to do things a lady must not—like hurl herself at him or, at the very least, run her fingers through that tousled, sun-bleached mane. No. A lady, certainly, had better make a dignified—and speedy—exit.

Grasping the door handle, she turned to leave.

"Why, you've only just come, Alexandra. 'They flee from me,' " he quoted. "But no, that's not right, is it? For you never 'did me seek,' did you? More's the pity."

"Do be quiet," she whispered. "Do you want everyone to hear you?"

"Why, they're all sound asleep, their consciences clear. Unlike yours and mine. But yes, my guardian angel," he went on, dropping his voice to a low timbre that sent a chill running down the back of her neck. "I take your meaning.

And if I promise to be very quiet, will you stay a minute and talk to me?"

Oh, how she wanted to stay, how she'd missed him. For all that he made her uncomfortable physically—and that was mainly the discomfort of trying to bring her desires into harmony with her morals—there was no one else with whom she could talk so easily. Because he knew her better than anyone else did . . . though she rather wished he didn't know her quite so well.

She looked down at her scanty attire and told herself to be sensible. "No. I only came for my book. I-I couldn't sleep." She glanced around the room, seeking the wayward volume.

"This one?" he asked, taking a familiar tome from the table near his head. *"Clarissa?* The interminable seduction? You are nearly at the end of it, I see." Idly he turned the pages. "Perhaps, as we're both wakeful, you might read to me."

"Don't be absurd." She was not sure what to do. She could not bring herself to go and take the book from him, nor did she think it advisable that he bring it to her. Nor did she wish to leave the room without it.

"Ah, I see the problem," he said, his eyes scanning her face. "What a thoughtless creature I am, to be sure. For here it is"—he consulted his pocket watch—"nearly half past one in the morning, and there are you in your dishabille, alone in a dim library with an arrant rogue. But see how simple it is? At this hour there's no one to notice the breach of decorum. There is my coat to protect your modesty. As to the rogue part—well, what dreadful thing do you think I'd dare attempt with the circumstances so very incriminating and my family only a shriek away?"

Putting the book down, he rose from the sofa. He took his coat from the chair, and held it up with a beckoning gesture.

She hesitated.

"Come, Miss Ashmore. Or are you afraid?"

Yes, actually, she was afraid. His effect on her was always unnerving, always dangerous. Still, he'd admitted that the risks were too great even for *him*. She put up her chin, crossed the room, and allowed him to help her on with his coat. He gestured towards the sofa, and she sat down gingerly.

She could not, however, suppress a gasp of shock when she saw him go to the door and turn the key in the lock. Grinning at her obvious alarm, he tossed the key to her. She caught it with trembling hands.

"That's in case there happen to be other insomniacs," he explained, as he pulled up a chair opposite her. "If we hear anyone coming, I shall crawl out the window while you take your time about going to the door. You would, of course, have locked it for fear of being disturbed by naughty gentlemen."

If she was uneasy at first, she forgot that as soon as he began talking, because immediately he set to telling her the true story of Randolph's elopement. Her surmises, she learned, had been correct. "But why," she asked, when he'd finished describing the elopement arrangements, "did you insist on going looking for him?"

"I couldn't rest easy until I was certain they were both in the coach and on their way. If the smallest thing went wrong, Randolph would have been helpless. Also, I was obliged to keep Henry Latham informed. We'd agreed, you see, that he'd handle the business end while I saw to the romance part of it."

"You mean he knew about the scheme all along?"

"He knew, thanks to my aunt, about your father's debt to George. He guessed about the romance sooner even than I did and must have dropped a hint to Aunt Clem when he wrote to her, for she dropped hints to me. None of which I picked up, I'm ashamed to admit. But when your Papa spoke that day about Randolph's breaking heart . . . well, to make a long story short, by the day of the picnic I'd not only got the truth out of Randolph, but also, in exchange for devising a workable elopement scheme, some important details regarding his father's practices. So off I dashed to Westford. Henry saw right off that mine was the best solution. It would have taken ages to reconcile his wife, and meanwhile George could have finally torn himself away from Yorkshire to force your marriage to his son. There was no time to be lost."

"So you had everything in hand before you left." There was a note of reproach in her voice.

Basil stared at the carpet. "I know. I should have told you. But the one time we were private—well, it all got driven out of my head. Then I made you hate me . . . and it was getting late. I should have been on my way hours before . . . and, well, I didn't tell you. I'm sorry. Truly I am. Because it would have spared you a deal of aggravation. If you'd known, you could have kept Will out of your hair easily enough, I'm sure."

She played with the key as she considered this. "I'd like to think so," she began slowly. "But it looks as though you've taken care of that, too, haven't you?" The green eyes fixed on him. "I should very much like to know what happened when you met up with him."

Mr. Trevelyan was evasive. He even looked uncomfortable, as he gave a highly edited account of his meeting with Lord Arden.

"What did you say to him?" she pressed. "Why did he avoid me all day?"

"I wish you wouldn't look at me that way. It turns my blood quite cold. I only had a serious discussion with him about the responsibilities of marriage, and he finally admitted he wasn't ready for them."

This, considering Will's impetuosity, she found a trifle hard to swallow. But then, was it so important? Basil had solved all her problems, disposed of all her fiancés. It was churlish to cavil at the means. "Never mind," she said with a small gesture of impatience. "It doesn't matter what you said. So long as I'm free of him."

"Ah, yes." Basil leaned forward a bit in his chair. "So that you may have your Season."

"Yes." She dropped her gaze to the key she held.

There was silence, and then his hand reached out to cover hers. "Then perhaps," he said softly, "we'll meet up with each other from time to time. Perhaps you'll be kind enough to dance with me now and again."

How easily he held her, his long fingers so lightly folded over her own, and how weak it made her feel. Her voice was brittle as she answered, "Why, yes, of course. I owe it all to you, don't I? And I've sat here all this time and never thanked you. I do thank you—"

He shook his head. "No. None of that. Not when I was only doing the little I know best."

She slipped her hand out from under his and stood up. "Well, I'm grateful all the same. Deeply grateful. I've never been free, not in six years at least. Now I am. I can't forget it. And so," she went on rather nervously, when he didn't respond, "I'll be bound to thank you from time to time, and you must endure it."

When she started to remove the coat, he seemed to collect himself from a daydream. He rose, too, moving to assist her. His hands touched her arms as the coat slipped from her shoulders, and she trembled slightly.

"Alexandra."

The sound was like a sigh, and she turned to look at him. The coat fell to the floor as he folded her in his arms. He kissed her, gently and briefly, and he drew away again before it occurred to her to *make* him do so.

He did not draw away entirely, however. His arms still held her, not so very close, but close enough so that she could feel the softness of his lawn shirt through the fragile barrier of her own flimsy garments. Close enough so that she was acutely conscious of the scent of him: clean and masculine and so comfortingly familiar. So comforting after all this time apart that it was quite impossible to break free. She felt so safe, so sheltered, so . . . *right* to be there, that any other possibility seemed quite wrong. That thought in itself was wrong, of course. It was only the spell he cast over her, and yet, to remain so . . . just another moment.

"I suppose," he said, rather sadly, "I'd better let you go."

"Yes, I think so," she answered just as sadly as she stared at the ruffles of his shirt front.

"Otherwise, I couldn't answer for the consequences." He did not release her.

"Yes." She didn't move.

"In another minute it would be too late." He sounded rather short of breath, and this for some reason irritated her.

"You always," she accused, "leave it up to *me*. But only after you make it—" She bit her lip.

He held her a little tighter. "Make it what?"

"So very difficult, Basil." Her green eyes met his.

Perhaps it was because she was breathless now as well, and because her heart beat so furiously, and because these conditions made it very difficult to think clearly. Whatever the reason, her hand strayed to his shirt, played with the ruffles briefly, then came to rest over his heart. It was thumping and that was somehow frustrating. Still, her hand remained where it was, and she went on, confusedly, "It's wicked of you . . . and—and unfair."

"Is it?" His lips brushed her forehead.

"Yes. And I don't see why I must always be the one to put a stop to—to everything. To get you out of the—the difficulties you get yourself into."

"Because I always get you out of yours. Because we've somehow got into the habit of looking out for each other. I wonder why," he murmured, drawing her closer still.

"Well, I'm not getting you out of this one," she answered with admirable severity, considering that she was talking into his neckcloth while he continued to drop light kisses in her hair. "You can just turn around and take yourself away."

"Can't," he whispered. "You have the key."

She was never sure afterward exactly how it happened, but one minute he was kissing her—*everywhere*, it seemed—and the next they had tumbled onto the great leather sofa. By that time, the notion of escaping was making less and less sense to her. How could one think of getting away from such caresses, when one's body with every passing moment desperately needed more of them? How could one wish to break free of that lean, muscular, beautiful body that claimed one so possessively? She covered his hand with hers. Fear and longing were mingled in the green eyes that searched his face.

"I won't hurt you," he whispered.

"No." Reason was fighting, desperately, to reassert itself. "No. I can't do this. No—I didn't mean—oh, Basil, please—have a little pity at least."

He had bent to kiss the hand clasping his, but now raised his head to look at her. His face was flushed, and his eyes, so softly golden before, were now so very bright. "Pity?" he repeated.

"I'm no m-match for you," she stammered. "You know that. It isn't fair."

He continued to gaze at her for the longest time, as though trying to interpret this rather inarticulate explanation. Then, very softly indeed, he said, "Ah, yes. My vast experience." His fingers slipped from her nerveless grasp and moved to push a tumbled curl away from her eye. "But about *you*, my love . . . when it comes to you, it seems I know nothing. I suppose," he added, with a wry smile, "we'll have to *deduce* everything." His head bent again, this time to the base of her throat, which he kissed very tenderly, sending tremors through her.

"Please."

She felt rather than heard his long, shuddering sigh as he moved away from her.

"Please," he muttered as he rose from the sofa. "To stop on a mere 'please.' How art the mighty fallen. Oh, Alexandra, you kill me with a word. No, don't look at me like that with those great, drowned eyes, or I shall wrestle my conscience down in an instant and we'll both be undone."

Afraid of what he might have seen in her face, she looked away quickly and struggled up to a sitting position. Only her mind had wanted him to stop. Her heart would have followed willingly, eagerly, wherever he'd led. All she'd offered up in defence of her virtue was "a mere please." For once—and to her shame—*he* had saved her from himself. No, not even that. "Both," he'd said. He'd saved himself as well.

"You'd better go," he was saying now. "I can't be a gentleman and help you up because I don't dare touch you again."

She was up and halfway to the door when she remembered it was locked. "The key," she said, turning back to him in embarrassment and dismay. She was even more dismayed when she noticed the expression on his face. A few moments ago he had appeared . . . well, troubled. Now his eyes gleamed in a too-familiar, wicked way, and his mouth wore that mocking smile. In the next instant, however, he had dropped to his knees to retrieve the key from under the sofa. In another minute the door was unlocked, and she was being propelled through it.

=== 19 ===

ALEXANDRA WINCED AS Emmy pulled the drapes open, and bright sunlight flooded the room. Morning already? But this was her assigned bed, and there was Emmy, pattering about the room, and a cup of steaming coffee on a tray on the bedstand. It all seemed perfectly normal . . . until, in a great, tumultuous flood, all that had happened—was it only a few hours ago?—came rushing into her consciousness vividly enough to set her face aflame. Quickly she turned to take the tray in her lap, but Emmy beat her to it.

"There, Miss," said the abigail, briskly. "Only do drink it up quicklike. Your Papa's waiting in his lordship's study to talk to you. And oh, Miss—he's dreadful cross."

Cross? She flushed again with guilt this time. But he could know nothing of *that*. It must be about Randolph. Perhaps he'd found out the truth somehow.

Hastily, Alexandra swallowed the coffee. She was no sooner out of bed than Emmy had hauled her to the washstand. In another minute the abigail was upon her again, pulling shift and dress over her head and fastening buttons and hooks with lightning speed.

The whole business of washing and dressing was accomplished so rapidly that Alexandra had barely, it seemed, opened her eyes before she was downstairs tapping on the study door. When she entered, she woke up quickly enough, for it was not just Papa standing there but Basil as well.

Her breath caught in her throat as she looked at him.

He'd seemed so different last evening, for a time at least. She remembered him, dishevelled and flushed, covering her with kisses and even laughing happily as he'd fallen onto the sofa with her. He'd seemed rather like an eager boy then.

Now, even casually dressed in his buckskins, he was so smart and elegant, his cat eyes cool and mocking, his lips pressed into a faint, amused smile. He looked what he was: a sophisticated man of the world who might have any woman he liked. Could any woman, regardless how sensible or intelligent, resist him for long? His gaze met hers then, and the intimate, knowing expression in those glowing amber eyes made her face burn. She looked away, moving towards the fireplace.

"Deuce take it," the baronet muttered, eyeing his daughter with vexation. "So that's how it is, is it?"

"How what is, Papa?" the daughter asked innocently. She had, however, to fold her hands very tightly to keep them from shaking.

"You. Him. Oh, damnation. Why can't a man ever get a little warning?"

Scrupulously avoiding Mr. Trevelyan's face, Alexandra asked her father what he meant.

"As if you didn't know. But *I* didn't, I admit. And when this—this—"

"Villain?" Basil offered, helpfully.

"When this villain saunters in and tells me he wants to marry you—"

Marry?

Considering the events of recent weeks, Miss Ashmore believed herself entirely immune to shock. She was not. She could not have been more stunned if Papa had hit her over the head with the poker she was now studying in numb fascination. Offered. He'd even gone right to Papa. Her mind was just beginning to resume operation as her father launched into a tirade.

"Of course, as you confide nothing to your poor Papa,

how am I to know? So, once again I'm made a fool of. I say, No, of course you won't have him. He insists that you will, and I tell him you won't. Not *my* daughter," the baronet went on sarcastically. "Not *my* Alexandra. She's much too clever to give herself over to the likes of him. And what happens but my brilliant offspring—too clever by half for her ignorant Papa—walks in and blushes like a green schoolgirl at the sight of him. Great Zeus, woman, haven't you any sense at all?"

In the rush of relief—of exaltation, even—Sense had been on the point of deserting her. But her father's words, for once in her life, made an impression. Give herself over to him. Oh, yes . . . easily, because she loved him so. To be his wife . . . *No*, she rebuked herself. Look how jealous and miserable she'd been yesterday, only imagining him flirting with other women. What she could imagine now was excruciating.

"Yes, of course I have sense, Papa," she answered steadily. "And I was not blushing like a schoolgirl—only flushed from running down to you in such a hurry. Of course the answer, as you said, is no." She turned briefly from the grate to throw Mr. Trevelyan a defiant look, but his expression made her turn away hastily.

The baronet's features relaxed. "No?"

"No."

"Well, then." Sir Charles turned to Basil. "There it is."

"No, it isn't." Mr. Trevelyan had moved nearer the door as this exchange was taking place. He now leaned back against it, his arms folded across his chest. "No is the wrong answer."

"I daresay you think it is," Sir Charles retorted with some impatience. "But she won't have you, and I certainly wouldn't consent unless she insisted—and that only to spare myself any more of her infernal wheedling. And so—"

"And so I'm afraid I shall have to tell you the truth," said Basil, quite calmly.

Panic swept through her. "Papa," she pleaded, "he's going to tell some lie. Make him go away."

"What truth? What lie?" the baronet demanded, glaring from one to the other.

"Nothing!" Alexandra shrieked.

"She's ruined," the calm voice went on. "I ruined her. Last night. In the li—"

"No!"

"Ruined her!" the baronet roared. His face contorted, turning nearly purple, as he launched himself at Mr. Trevelyan. "I'll kill you!" he screamed. But he found he couldn't kill the wretch because his exasperating daughter had thrown herself in the way.

"No, Papa. Stop please!" She stood in front of Basil, shielding him. "The servants will hear you. Of course it's not true. You mustn't let him provoke you. He's only made this up to blackmail me, Papa." She went on babbling protestations, which was monstrous difficult when Mr. Trevelyan's finger was tracing a lazy path down her back. She sprang away when she felt a slight pressure at the base of her spine. "Stop it!" she hissed.

Luckily, Sir Charles was no longer looking at them. He was glowering at the carpet, shaking his head. "If it is a lie," he growled, "I shall call him out."

"I see your point, sir. Perhaps, then, I was exaggerating. Perhaps she isn't ruined. Still, the circumstances were exceedingly compromising—"

"Basil!"

Sir Charles considered for a moment. He looked from his daughter whose cheeks were very pink to Clementina's dreadful nephew whose colour had also deepened.

"I see," he said slowly. "I am not such a fool as all that. Why," he demanded, "would any rakehell in his senses tell your father such a thing, truth or not? Only," he answered himself, "if he was set on marrying you. If that's the case, you'd better have him, Alexandra. Either way he'll make your life a misery, but married to him you can return the favour. I wish you joy of each other, indeed I do. It's just as you deserve."

He nodded to himself with grim satisfaction, deaf to his daughter's continued pleadings and protestations.

"No, madam," he said as he absently patted the hand clutching his sleeve. "I don't want to hear any more of it. You have tired me half to death for the past six years. Now you have my leave to tire *him* for the next sixty. Let *him* worry about your admirers and infatuations from now on." He shook off his daughter's hand and marched to the door.

When Basil stepped aside to let him pass, she attempted to slip out as well.

"No," said the baronet. "You had better remain and reconcile yourself to your affianced husband. You will marry him, Alexandra—and so I shall inform your god-mother. I daresay it's no news to her, the interfering jade. When you join us—both of you—I expect you to conduct yourselves with some decorum for once. I've had enough scenes for this millenium, I think." With surprising dignity, Sir Charles took himself out of the room.

When the door had closed on her Papa, Miss Ashmore turned on her latest fiancé, her green eyes blazing. "I hate you," she said. "I shall always hate you. And I will never—*never*, do you hear me?—marry you."

"No, you don't, and yes, you will," he answered composedly. "Now come, Alexandra, say something kind to me, for you've hurt my feelings dreadfully." He moved to take her in his arms, but she spun away out of his reach.

"How dare you say such things to Papa?"

"At this point, I'd dare anything. Do you think I mean to let my aunt take you back to London, where you can acquire another set of beaux for me to dispose of? I should think not. Even I would like a bit of rest now and then. I should vastly prefer resting with you in my arms," he added, very tenderly.

This brought forcibly to mind some rather delicious moments when she'd been nestled in his arms. As she felt herself weakening, she grew correspondingly cross. She moved away to take up her post before the fireplace again and frowned into the grate. "That's the worst way of offering for a woman I've ever heard," she told the grate.

"If I'd asked in the normal way, would you have accepted me?"

Yes, she thought, because I'm a fool. "No," she answered. "I couldn't. I can't."

"Why? I mean, besides the fact that you solemnly promised ages ago to jilt me."

She shot him an exasperated glance, but his horrid self-assurance was replaced by a bleak look that knocked all her angry retorts out of her. "It doesn't matter," she said.

In a few steps he crossed the room to stand at her shoulder. "It does matter. Tell me why. And tell me the truth, for once."

She was silent for a moment. There was an ache in her throat, a terrible ache. Really, it should not be so very painful, this process of sparing oneself future pain. Nonetheless, the tears welled up and trembled on her lashes as though to keep the ache company.

"Why?" he asked again. "You might do me the courtesy of telling me why you're so determined to make me wretched."

"You? It's you who'll make *me* wretched," she blurted out past the ache and the tears. "Because there'll always be one temptation or another you can't resist. Oh, Basil, maybe now you think you want me, but in time you'll be bored. How am I to bear that?"

"I see. You're fully convinced that I should make a thoroughly unreliable, unfaithful, neglectful husband."

She nodded miserably.

"Whereas you, on the other hand, would be the ideal wife. Sweet and biddable, never thinking of manipulating her besotted spouse to get her own way. The very soul of honesty who'd scorn to tell her husband even the smallest fib. Certainly he need never worry about all the eager gentlemen clustered about his wife. Your spouse would never have to live in your pocket, for fear of other gentlemen's dishonourable intentions."

Her eyes, still fixed on the grate, opened very wide.

"No, really," he continued, "there's nothing at all daunting in the prospect of marrying the most desirable woman in England, not even though she happens to be dreadfully clever and manipulative besides. Not at all. I'm certain Napoleon's Grand Army might have managed such a business if, that is, they kept well together."

"What," she asked fiercely as she turned to him, "are you implying?"

"I wasn't implying anything. I was telling you straight out. The idea of marrying you frightens me out of my wits. Unfortunately, I'm so desperately in love with you that I must or shoot myself."

Love. He'd spoken tender words last night, the sweet words that came so easily to him, but he'd never uttered a syllable about love.

He was still speaking. "I offer you my very small, very vulnerable, fragile, nearly breaking heart. You trample on it, and remind me that I'm a villain. Well, so what if I am? I'm the villain who's compromised you—not once but several times—and I'm the one who loves you." He pulled her to him. "And I'm the one you're stuck with, because your Papa says so. I wish you'd stop quarrelling with me and kiss me." He must have thought better of it, because he kissed *her* instead.

Recognising that the odds were against her, Miss Ashmore very sensibly yielded to her opponent. In the true British spirit of good sportsmanship, she returned his kiss with enthusiasm. The victor generously returned hers, so she was obviously obliged to return his. So it continued for some minutes until the two found themselves in danger of committing a great impropriety. To her credit, Miss Ashmore became conscious of the peril in time and pulled away from him.

He swore under his breath. "What a curst business this is," he muttered. "Why did I have to fall in love with a proper young lady and be doomed to these furtive escapades in other people's houses? Halls. Libraries. Studies. What next? Shall we rendezvous in the kitchens after midnight? Or will you meet me in the stables?"

"The stables?" she repeated, greatly indignant.

"Sorry. I wasn't thinking. Or I wasn't thinking what I ought. The trouble is, I paced the library all night, and it was cold and lonely without you. I missed you horribly. Then I had to wait ages before your Papa was up. The waiting was horrible. I nearly hung myself."

She'd been about to read him a lecture about his fiancée not being a common lightskirt to be tumbled about in hayracks. The lecture flew out of her head as she gazed up wonderingly into those beautifully wicked amber eyes. "Were you lonely for me, Basil? Really?"

"Good God. For such an intelligent woman you can be remarkably stupid, my love. Did you think I wanted you to leave?"

"You were very abrupt, Basil, and you did push me out the door."

"The only way I know to resist temptation is to remove it. That should have been obvious. If it wasn't—well, I take back what I said earlier. You *are* stupid. You're the stupidest woman it's ever been my misfortune to fall in love with." To emphasise the point, he kissed her once more very lingeringly. As this promised to bring them both into difficulties again, she pushed him away.

"We can't stay here all day," she warned, as she stooped to gather up her wayward hairpins. "Papa's expecting us to join him and Aunt Clem."

Basil relieved his feelings with a few more quiet oaths as he helped her find her hairpins and restore herself to a semblance of respectability. Finally, the two went forth to face his aunt.

Whatever story was told to Lady Bertram and Sir Charles must have been satisfactory. In another hour, host, hostess, and guests were gathered in the drawing room, listening as Sir Charles—with fiendish relish—informed one and all that his daughter and Clementina's nephew were to be shackled for the rest of their natural, or unnatural was more like it, lives.

Lord Tuttlehope was so astonished that he forgot to blink. "*Marry* her?" he said to his wife. "Is that what he says?"

"Yes, dear," Alicia answered with a giggle. "Isn't it delicious?"

Evidently her husband didn't think so, for when he later offered his congratulations to his friend, Lord Tuttlehope's speech had the lugubrious ring of condolences.

"You might look a little more cheerful when you wish me happy, Freddie," said Basil biting back a grin. "I'm not going to be hung, you know—only married."

Lord Tuttlehope appeared to think it was quite the same thing. He manufactured an awful smile. "But Trev. You? Can't believe it. Sorry." Distractedly he put out his hand. "Happy. And all that."

Mr. Trevelyan returned the handshake with all due solemnity.

"But Trev. Thought you hated her."

"Well, I don't. That wouldn't be a very promising way to commence wedded life, would it? Come, Freddie, don't look so tragic. You're married and happy, aren't you?"

"Course I'm happy. But you're different, Trev," Lord Tuttlehope noted mournfully.

"Yes," Basil agreed. "So is *she*."

Lord Arden, for other reasons, looked equally pitying.

"Poor fellow," he said, clapping Basil on the shoulder. "You should have heeded your own advice, I think." He glanced past his erstwhile rival towards Miss Ashmore who was surrounded by a group of happy ladies, including his irritating sister. "Still, it's a beautiful trap for all that.

Indeed, I do wish you the best of luck, Trev." His gaze turned back to Basil, looking, he thought, rather feral. "You'll need it, you know. Just as you said. Do not be surprised if you see me in my hunting pinks." With that and a brief, mocking bow the marquess left to offer his best wishes to the bride-to-be.

Mr. Trevelyan smiled easily enough as he turned to his cousin who had joined him, champagne bottle in hand. "What a troublesome business this marriage business is, Edward. I'm not even wed yet, and the gentlemen are already announcing their designs on my wife."

"Very gracious of them it is, I must say," was the dry reply. "Will takes his defeat philosophically enough. I'd have thought he'd rather put a bullet through your scheming brain. But tell me," the earl went on, dropping his voice as he refilled his and his cousin's glasses, "what did happen when you met up with him? Did you treat him to one of your gypsy fortune-teller performances like the one you used on my wife? One of your twisted tragic tales?"

"Cuz, you cut me to the quick. I simply told the man the Truth, plain and unvarnished."

"Did you now? Well, it was what he wanted after all. He didn't need even to wring it out of you, did he? Still, I do wonder how you managed to convince that lovely, intelligent girl to trust her future to you. But why do I ask? 'Thou hast damnable iteration, and art indeed able to corrupt a saint.' "

"How you flatter me, my lord."

"For the first and I hope the last time. Well then, cuz," said Lord Hartleigh, raising his glass, "here's to your damnable iteration or the Truth or whatever it is. And though you don't deserve it a bit, I do wish you happy."

20

A MONTH LATER a newlywed couple sat in a large bed in the most luxurious bedroom of a select, outrageously expensive inn some miles from London. The groom, still partially dressed, leaned back against the pillows inspecting the ring on his wife's finger. She sat watching him, her chestnut curls all unpinned and tumbling in gay abandon about her face.

"I have a wife," Basil said at last, softly and wonderingly. "How very odd."

She looked a little anxious as she asked, "Is it, dear? I know you never meant to have one."

"Didn't I? Well, how stupid of me, to be sure. When I think what might have happened if you hadn't managed to seduce me that night in the library—"

"I did not," she interrupted indignantly, "seduce you."

"You would have, if I hadn't such a scrupulous regard for my virtue. You knew I was exhausted, and therefore in a vulnerable condition, and you attempted to take selfish advantage of my weakness."

"Oh, I see. And which weakness was that? You have so many it's hard to tell."

"A weakness," he said, bringing the hand he held to his lips, "for naughty chestnut curls that will not stay properly pinned. A weakness for green eyes." He kissed each fingertip in turn.

"What a shallow fellow you are, sir. Any woman might have seduced you—and no doubt will, in future."

"Oh, ye of little faith. To speak so, after you've done everything possible to enslave me utterly." Abruptly he dropped her hand, got off the bed, and picked up his coat from the floor.

"What are you doing, Basil? You're not leaving—"

"Hardly." He fished out a much-creased letter from the coat pocket and carried it back to the bed with him. As his wife watched with growing impatience, he settled himself comfortably again.

"Well?"

"Well." He dangled the folded letter before her eyes. "Do you know what that is?"

"Whatever it is, it appears to have been rather knocked about. What is it, Basil? A love letter from one of your high flyers?"

"You might say that."

As he slowly unfolded the sheets, she gasped. "That's my writing," she cried. "What is it?"

" 'My dearest Aunt Clem,' " he began, " 'I am so sorry to trouble you with this absurdity, but matters here have, I think, got out of hand—' " He broke off as his wife tried to snatch the letter from him. "Oh, no," he told her, holding it out of her reach, "I haven't kept it so safely and tenderly all this time that you might tear it to pieces, my darling. Besides, I know it by heart."

"Where did you get that?"

"It was sent me. By my dearest Auntie."

"Aunt Clem sent it to you? When?"

"When I was in Greece."

Though she was a married lady of some hours, Alexandra could still blush. Recalling some of the comments in that letter, she did so now. "In Greece," she echoed faintly.

"Yes. Aunt Clem is monstrous underhanded, you know. Anyhow," he went on, allowing the letter to drop gently to the floor, "I read it and was lost utterly. Your brutally comic description of Randolph and his odious family. As you listed everything that you'd tried and failed with your

Papa—well, I felt rather a kinship with you, you know. And then I saw you, dirty and bedraggled in that crowded room. You were so beautiful in spite of it. You knew immediately what I was about and played your part so well. You acted to admiration, my love. I very nearly believed my own lie. Naturally, when I kissed you, I sealed my fate. What could be more romantic?"

His beloved was staring at the bedpost. "You don't mean to say that Aunt Clem deliberately—but no, how could she? How could she possibly guess—"

"Oh, she didn't guess, my love. She knew we were meant for each other. Aunt Clem sees all, knows all. And knowing her, she had Maria in it as well. My precious," he cried as he flung himself back upon the pillows, his hand clutched to his breast, "we're the victims of a conspiracy. You and I—as wicked a set of connivers as ever walked this great island—the innocent victims of an unscrupulous pair of matchmakers. *Matchmakers*, Alexandra. How lowering."

The bride transferred her gaze from the bedpost to her groom. "Lowering? I should say so. I never had the trace of a suspicion. Good grief. And your aunt let me go through all that horrendous business."

"Hasn't a conscience, dear. Runs in the family."

"Is that so?" The green eyes narrowed. "Just how long have you known about this?"

"If you keep on looking at me like that I shall scream. It makes my blood curdle. Really it does." He manoeuvred himself into more comfortable proximity to his lovely wife. "I assure you I feel as stupid as you do. It never occurred to me. In all my frenzy of jealousy and scurrying hither and yon and plotting, there was no room in my brain for my aunt. Once again she has triumphed over me. I suppose I shall have to endure it, just as I endured my gloomy exile." In proof of this stoic determination, he dropped several lingering kisses upon his wife's creamy shoulder.

"Poor Basil. It was none of your doing, was it? But all these wicked females taking advantage."

He murmured an unintelligible reply from the nape of her neck.

"It was I who trapped you, was it? Caught you in my wicked toils? Compromised you?"

"Well, I helped," he admitted. "Because I'm so gallant, you know."

"Oh yes, poor dear."

"At any rate, thanks to Aunt Clem, I've had a month to become reconciled to my fate. We could have had a perfectly acceptable ceremony the next day. Edward had only to use his influence for a special licence. But no. A big wedding, says my aunt, is the only recompence for not giving you a proper comeout."

"It has been a very long time," said his wife. "I've nearly forgotten what it was like exactly. Compromising you, I mean."

"What a shocking poor memory you've got, madam. You've even forgotten that you never did accomplish my ruination. I suppose," he breathed, as he pulled her face down to his, "I shall have to spend the rest of my life helping you remember these . . . matters."

She sighed, and in a very bored and weary sort of way, agreed, "Yes, my love, and how very tiresome for you—"

She was permitted to say no more . . . and very soon thereafter was so agreeably occupied that she forgot what she'd intended to say.